THE SINNER'S CONGREGATION

Martin Lomax has, through family connections, become the reluctant owner of the Bali Hotel after several years of pleasing himself abroad. He finds that life is fun; and is entertained every night by the company of his customers: Alice Chetwynd Stapleton, a colourful widow whose acid conversation sears many an evening; Adam, a man who can do almost anything except make money or find a wife; and Rodney Pym, who gets richer and richer but has never recovered from losing his first wife to a fifteen-stone transvestite.

Suddenly, Martin is horrified to discover that an ogre from his past has booked into the hotel. He recovers quickly, though, and decides that the new arrival hasn't been delivered into the professional care of the Bali by accident . . .

The Sinner's Congregation

Guy Bellamy

CORGI BOOKS

THE SINNER'S CONGREGATION

A CORGI BOOK 0 552 12289 0

Originally published in Great Britain by Martin Secker & Warburg Limited

PRINTING HISTORY
Secker & Warburg edition published 1982
Corgi edition published 1983

A portion of this book originally appeared in *Punch*

This book is set in 10/11 Plantin

Corgi Books are published by
Transworld Publishers Ltd.,
Century House, 61–63 Uxbridge Road,
Ealing, London W5 5SA

Made and printed in Great Britain by
Hunt Barnard Printing Ltd., Aylesbury, Bucks.

FOR CAROLE
for her birthday

Wherever God erects a house of prayer,
The Devil always builds a chapel there;
And 'twill be found, upon examination,
The latter has the larger congregation.
Daniel Defoe

People who have never tried it
have no idea how pleasant
being nasty can be.
Wilfred Sheed
(The Good Word And
Other Words)

Am always a perfectly safe man to tell
any dirt to as it goes in one ear and out
my mouth.
Ernest Hemingway

Part One

Friday

1

It is difficult to love the human race when you have watched a roomful of people eating as often as I have, but given the price that most of them are prepared to pay others for providing their food I've learned to tolerate their hoggish ways. My many attempts to become obscenely rich have been abortive and often farcical, but this beautiful hotel, small and demanding though it is, does seem to be the next best thing to an oil well in your back yard. At night, for instance, when we are all in bed, I never fail to remind myself that money from the other recumbent bodies is slowly dripping into my pocket, and if I have sold them enough expensive drinks before they retire they won't even want the breakfast for which they have already paid. It is a sad morning when I don't wake up £200 richer than when I fell asleep.

I became the proprietor of this gold-mine two years ago on my thirty-sixth birthday. My parents handed over the keys and retired to the red hills of Devon, their departure having been delayed for several years by my reluctance to take over the responsibilities of business. They finally bluffed me into action by threatening to put the hotel on the market. The prospect of my last best chance of affluence vanishing at auction cleared my mind wonderfully. I bought a suit and moved in.

The Bali Hotel is, I am glad to say, hard to find. It stands — pale pink-washed walls, thatched roof and even, I am afraid, honeysuckle in copious quantities over the door — at the end of a long country lane which plunges down through the trees off one of the new dual carriageways which scar the North Downs. It was originally built as a monks' retreat and later became a staging post for travellers across southern England.

On a beautiful reach of a river (I am quoting now from my own brochure) with a quaint riverside garden and ample car-park space, it has twelve guest-rooms with colour televisions and bathrooms *en suite*. This same brochure, written one Sunday afternoon with the assistance of half a bottle of claret, urges would-be customers to 'enjoy the countryside, observe the wildlife, fish for trout or salmon, or play golf on one of the many local courses'. There are no salmon, and the wildlife consists of a few bedraggled moorhens and coots, and a battalion of mallards who turn their green heads to one side and glare at you with one eye.

The interior of the hotel, it says here, has been extensively and tastefully renovated and great care has been taken to maintain the original character and charm of the building, while combining the best of modern comforts and facilities. What this means is that you each have your own bathroom and lavatory, but the roof is still thatched.

Chaucer's pilgrims, medieval bargees and William Cobbett himself passed this way; today's guest is more likely to be a prosperous middle-class businessman in a Volvo.

Of course the name is absurd — an uncharacteristically moonstruck idea of my mother's, after watching the musical *South Pacific* — but it is in so many guidebooks now that to change it would be counter-productive: the Bali has a reputation.

Our guests come from two quite different categories. The weekend arrivals are looking for a romantic break in the country. They don colourful weekend clothes and wander out on to the lawn taking deep breaths as if inhaling fresh air is some bucolic eccentricity which they will try just this once. On Sunday mornings they stroll down to the river which every so often floods my garden and then my patio and, twice, my cellar, and, armed with *The Complete Guide to British Wildlife*, will tell me about the willowherb or angelica they have found. Sometimes the more adventurous among them stride off into the pine and heather country with binoculars and walking-sticks and return limping and blistered.

The weekday guests are different. Mostly they are businessmen or men who are on courses locally and whose bills are paid by their firms. They are valued customers: it is surprising how extravagant a man can be when someone else is paying his bill.

I preside over this modest enterprise with ill-concealed disdain, resenting equally the voracious demands of my customers and the financial shackles which bind me here. But the plentiful flaws in my temperament have, quite accidentally, combined to produce the right demeanour for a *maître d'hôtel*: here in the catering business the unsure customer is perversely reassured by being patronized — he gets his confidence from yours.

My biggest problem, predictably, has been the staff, and in the early days I thought it would defeat me. I have had to grab youngsters off the street, hose them down, dress them up, and call them waiters: I have had chambermaids who earned more in the bedrooms than I ever paid them; I have had a chef who, in a unique feat of culinary kamikaze, set fire to himself in the kitchen and left the pay-roll with third-degree burns; I have had a receptionist who took more than she received. I solved the problem by firing most of them and doubling the pay of those who remained. I now have a trim staff of three and a half. This half is Mrs Newman, who comes in when she is needed.

My full-time chef — double pay and a free flat on the top floor — is a young man called Scott, with sad eyes, a Samurai moustache and a Yamaha motor-bike which he rarely gets the chance to use. My receptionist and waitress is his wife Judy. They are saving up to buy their own hotel, and with the money they are earning they will soon be able to afford this one.

The third member of the team is Lisa, who is chambermaid in the morning, topping up the tea-making machines in the bedrooms, and barmaid at night. She is never slow to complain about her hours, her conditions or her wages, but when

I call her Moaner Lisa she smiles enigmatically, unaware of my spelling. Lisa is a very bright twenty-four-year-old and I have never found out what event in her past drove her into the seclusion of the Bali. If it was the search for a husband she was labouring under a mighty handicap: body odour. I could smell her when she was behind me. In the early days, before I realized how valuable she was, I risked offence by asking what the smell was. She surprised me by naming an expensive perfume. It was only afterwards that I realized that the perfume wasn't neat, but diluted by the sweat of days. Not surprisingly, I never saw her with a man.

'Your epitaph will be returned unopened,' I told her once when she was drunk.

'Or laid at last,' she suggested brightly.

In this dazzingly efficient team I am the utility player who plugs all gaps. To have attained the heady status of reserve chambermaid at this stage of my life is something that never ceases to irk me.

I am sustained by gossip, an unfairly maligned commodity in some circles but much valued at the Bali Hotel. The items are passed around quite shamelessly, often exchanged for another, and if I am not the first to know, I am always the second. I know awful truths about some customers — domestic, financial, medical, sexual — that they don't know themselves, or certainly don't know that I know. Compulsive gossiping is a sign of a lively curiosity (it's a sadly self-centred man who displays no interest in other people's lives) and there is great satisfaction to be derived from passing information on. 'A secret kept is a secret wasted', is the working motto here.

The bar at the Bali has a full on-licence, which means that non-residents can get stoned here too. For a discriminating and perennially thirsty section of the people who live in the surrounding countryside it is their bar.

At the head of this group of dedicated topers is Alice Chetwynd Stapleton, whose acid conversation, I recall with relish, has seared many an evening. Mrs Stapleton, a widow of sixty, lives in a small Tudor cottage up the lane with a black labrador called Boz and a hot line to the local betting shop. I give her meat for her dog but never for herself. She is a militant vegetarian. Early every evening she arrives in the bar for a cocktail or two — a white lady or a sidecar — then leaves to eat, before returning later to attack a bottle of gin. She is my favourite customer.

On that fateful Friday evening she sailed in wearing a long cotton shirt, with a sumptuous floral design, which hung outside wide, brown trousers. Over the shirt was a long knitted waistcoat equipped with some much-used pockets. She never carried a bag. Her most delightful idiosyncrasy, however, was her collection of cheap wigs, which she wore in erratic rotation to conceal very short grey hair. They were often lopsided and sometimes removed. She had an urchin cut and a pageboy cut. Tonight it was just plain curly.

'Hit me with a Gordon's,' she said, dragging a stool noisily to where she wanted it at the bar. 'Will you have one, Martin?'

'Not yet,' I told her.

'Has it ever occurred to you that we have all lived before, been sentenced on the day of judgement to hell — and this is it?'

I handed her the gin. 'Do I take it that you've had a bad day, Alice?' I asked.

'No worse than usual. The dog's sick, the television's packed up and I lost five pounds on a horse. An average sort of day.'

'In that case let me pay for the gin. Alcohol is a mood-changing drug.'

'Drugs are what young people have,' said Mrs Stapleton. 'I have a drink.' She sipped it thoughtfully. 'Young people — promiscuous, selfish, unscrupulous, lazy and weak. I sometimes think that a hundred years of free education has produced a generation with the moral fibre of the monkey-house.'

The reactionary sentiments of Mrs Stapleton were one of the great joys of conversation at the Bali. It was dealt with by

15

ridicule or agreement or, in the case of Adam, frenzied argument.

'It hasn't been the same since the British flag came down in Delhi,' I said.

'You're taking the mickey, Martin, but I was there. The fourteenth of August 1947. I shall never forget it.'

'Clearly,' I murmured.

'You're too young to remember it, too young to remember the war.'

'I remember the war very well,' I said. 'I didn't see a banana until I was seven.'

'You didn't allow it to scar your soul, I trust?'

Before I could answer this, Adam came in. Adam is my most regular customer. He is a tall, lean, good-looking man of about forty with black wavy hair and eyes that suggest that life has hurt him in some way.

I don't believe that Adam is his real name — he resembles too closely the star of an old western series on television who was called Adam, and I was once told that he had taken the sobriquet gladly. Perhaps his real name is Cuthbert.

Adam is a man of protean talents but little means. He is always having money-making ideas that don't make any money. There must have been some artistic training buried in his past because he occasionally talks about paintings he has done and painters he admires. But the only painting I have seen him do is people's houses. He can also write poetry, build a wall, change a door, repair a car, bake bread, catch trout, ride horses, play the violin and administer the kiss of life. There seem occasionally to be only two things that Adam can't do: make money and find a wife.

His quest for a wife had now taken on a slightly desperate air: phone numbers that obviously promised nothing but rejection were frantically sought and noted; ladies only temporarily unattached or not unattached at all were cornered and flattered; trysts were made, secret assignations kept. But no joyous announcements followed this urgent activity, no visits to jewellers, no invitations to church. He lives alone in a very small, scantily furnished flat attached to a rather large, luxuriously furnished house that is hidden beneath the trees on the hill between my hotel and the main road. And he always denies that he is looking for a wife.

'Hallo, pal,' he said, sliding on to a stool. 'Sell me a pint.' He was wearing a clean white shirt and dirty, paint-stained jeans. He turned to Mrs Stapleton, with whom he was continually engaged in verbal warfare. 'Hallo, Alice. Give me a kiss. You know that you secretly lust after my virile young body.'

'No, I don't,' said Mrs Stapleton. 'In fact it was apathy at first sight.'

'Have a gin?'

'Just a large one.'

I fetched their drinks and refused one for myself. If I took all the drinks I am offered I would have been dead a long time ago.

'When are you going to get a proper job, Adam,' said Mrs Stapleton, 'and stop all this piddling about?'

I had a lot of sympathy for Adam, having done my share of drifting over the years. I drifted into the hotel in the first place because my parents owned it, and at twenty-eight I didn't so much drift out of it as rush out in a panic at the thought of a lifetime tied to the Bali. I also became mildly neurotic at the grey mattress of cloud that seemed to be anchored permanently over the British Isles. I drifted to Europe, and it was eight years before I returned to run the hotel on my own.

At first I had the crazy idea of trying to earn a living as a photographer in Paris, but the huge candle-lit aisles of Notre Dame were crowded not with worshippers but with tourists who carried their own cameras round their necks and I moved south, looking for the sun. I reached La Rochelle, but the weather was English so I caught a train to Biarritz and spent a lonely week there vainly looking for work.

I crossed the border — the further south I went the warmer I became — and wound up eventually in Barcelona. It was no easier to find work there and I was wondering whether to fly home one day, sitting in Los Caracoles, just

17

off the Ramblas, when I met a girl. She was a very thin, pale-faced girl with huge spectacles, and when she wasn't eating she had her nose in a book. It was in English and I was hungry for company so I asked her where she was going.

'The Balearic archipelago,' she said, looking up only briefly. It was some moments before I realized where she meant.

'Holiday?' I asked.

She looked up again, emphasizing quite adequately how unwelcome my intrusion was.

'I'm going to see Robert Graves,' she said.

'What's that?' I said. 'Some fancy cemetery?'

'There are no cemeteries in Majorca,' she replied, ignoring my little joke. 'That's the first thing an intelligent visitor notices. Not that Majorca gets many intelligent visitors these days.'

It sounded like my sort of place. Two hours later I was sitting, drink in hand, on the Trans-Mediterranean Ferry, reading a booklet about Majorca's medieval history while my former companion sat out on the deck reading Proust. The tiny island had mountains that were higher than any in Britain and orange groves where trees a thousand years old were still bearing fruit. I had fallen for it before I arrived.

Majorca reciprocated by providing work. Within days I was employed in an underground bowling alley, a job I eventually relinquished in search of fresh air. I sold tickets for trips round Palma Bay in a glass bottomed boat, and moved on from there to manage one of the island's hundreds of discothèques where holidaymakers paid absurd prices for imitation champagne, and profits enabled me not only to survive but save. One evening sixteen Germans and fifteen English rugby players decided to re-enact World War Two. The ensuing carnage, according to a newspaper report, made that war look like a game of croquet. I thought this a mite hyperbolic, but it took me four hours to clean up the blood and by the time I finished the police had closed the place down for six months, putting seals on the door which meant that not even the owners were allowed in. My caravan rolled on.

The people that I met at this time, mostly respectable Britons on a two-week break from the mouse race, occasionally rebuked me for lacking ambition but I had the three oldest ambitions in the world: life, liberty and the pursuit of happiness. The zeal with which I sought to realize them would, in a glassy skyscraper in the City, have produced a seat on the board within a year. But life is too short for a seat on the board and usually much shorter if you get one.

I went to work in a bar at Maravillas, serving drinks at hours unknown to the lazy barmen of my cloudy homeland. The owner was a Scotsman who needed capital to build the beer garden which would make his venture profitable. I provided it and we became partners. This enabled me to swim, sail and fish as well as sell drinks and food. I made the most of my time, knowing that one day the Bali would reclaim me.

All of these endeavours have left me with a million pesetas in the Banco Hispano Americano in what was then called the Paseo Generalismo Franco in Palma. But what is a million pesetas today? It wouldn't even buy me a good car.

It was the first evening, the Friday evening, of the late summer bank holiday and I was secretly nurturing some earth-shaking plans for it. Before the weekend was through I was going to stun my staff, delight Mrs Stapleton and demoralize Adam by becoming engaged. I was looking forward to it with quiet excitement. I could already hear the happy laughter and taste the champagne.

Of course, if I had known what the weekend held for me I would have shut up the hotel that evening and hurried away to pass the holiday in someone else's, preferably in the Ellice Islands.

I left Lisa to handle the bar and went away to check on the business. Half a dozen people were eating in the restaurant and I wandered round in there for a while checking on the cleanliness of the cutlery, the cloths and the nearly new menus. The restaurant is on the left as you come in the front door and the bar on the right. Facing you is the reception desk and I sat there flipping through the books. A party of six men

19

were due in from Yorkshire that evening, presumably planning a weekend of fishing or golf, and two couples, with their guide books, were expected from London. It looked like a quiet weekend.

I went into the kitchen and made myself an omelette while Scott prepared something more lavish for the paying guests. It is surprising how your appetite shrinks when you are surrounded by food and I once considered running a novel course for slimmers. All they would do was work in my kitchen for a month.

'You keep a dog and bark yourself,' said Scott, watching me turn the omelette.

'You under-rate yourself,' I said. 'Why do you think I pay you so much money?'

'Because I work every bloody bank holiday,' he said. 'Put some pepper in it.'

When I returned to the bar Adam was attempting to allay Mrs Stapleton's suspicions that his life lacked purpose by outlining his latest plan for untold wealth.

'I'm going to be a writer,' he said.

Only a week earlier he had told us that he was going to be a dealer, a title which, apparently, covered a confusing variety of activities and meant that you didn't pay income tax. On his first day in his new role he had taken his battered van to an auction just outside London and returned triumphantly with a hundredweight of used gym shoes, some industrial vacuum cleaners, ten stainless-steel hand-basins, two dozen fire extinguishers and a weighing machine. His attempts to shift this haul at a marginal profit to himself had not so far been successful and it was now cluttering up his flat. Stage two of his career as a dealer was to have involved the purchase of fifty window frames that were coming up at a local auction, but as his first bizarre consignment remained unsold he had what he now described in his new businessman's jargon as a negative cash balance.

'Writing requires no capital,' he said. 'For someone like me that's a considerable attraction.'

'That's probably why Shakespeare took it up,' suggested

Mrs Stapleton. 'Biros must have cost next to nothing in Stratford in the sixteenth century.'

'And what are you going to do with a hundredweight of used gym shoes?' I asked.

'What I thought I might do was give them to a school for the mentally handicapped and then write a short story about the whole episode.'

'You could call it "The Used Gym Shoes",' said Mrs Stapleton. 'It's a title that's redolent of something.'

'Why don't you give them the two dozen fire extinguishers as well?' I asked. 'It could make a sequel.'

'I can see that this new literary career has a lot of fans already,' said Adam. 'I shall continue undiscouraged. I wrote my first story this afternoon and it's a stunner. I'm going to make money and have more time for fun. Increased means and increased leisure are the civilizers of man.'

'Old Adam,' said Mrs Stapleton. 'The man who put the F in philosophy.'

I served them drinks and had one myself. Slowly, as various television programmes came to an end, people were strolling out for their first weekend drink and Lisa was kept busy down the bar. When the orders stopped, she washed glasses beneath the counter.

Through the front window I could see a red Citröen gliding slowly down the lane. It turned into my car park, and seemed to be packed with people. A rear door opened first and a man fell out as if he had been cramped up for too long. He helped a second man out and then a third. A door at the front opened and as more men appeared the first opened the boot and produced suitcases and golf clubs.

'That must be the Yorkshire party,' I said to Lisa. 'They have rooms two to seven. Can you show them up?'

She went off to greet the guests and I found myself facing one of our more boring customers, a retired school-teacher who seemed to wilt physically if he couldn't hear the sound of his own voice. Today, once I had sold him a whisky and water, he wanted to tell me of his experience that afternoon when he had taken his car to be serviced, or cleaned, or resprayed — I didn't listen until my favourite phrase came drifting over the counter.

'To cut a long story short,' he said, and I smiled encouragingly. In a world in which people are mysteriously becoming more long-winded, and in a job where an attentive ear is the most appreciated commodity a customer can be offered, there is no single phrase in the English language that can lighten my heart as much as 'to cut a long story short'. It brings a smile of admiration to my face.

'What happened?' I asked.

'I refused to pay.'

'I don't blame you,' I said.

'Would you have paid?'

'I would not,' I said. 'They could whistle for it.'

'That's what I told my wife. They can whistle for it.' He was delighted that I shared his indignation.

'What would you do about it?' he asked.

This was difficult. But not too difficult.

'Excuse me, there's a gentleman waiting to be served,' I told him. Adam was brandishing an empty glass and demanding a lager. I took the glass to the pump but it produced only froth and noise.

Lisa came back.

'They said they are big drinkers,' she said. 'And two of them fancy me.'

'That's good,' I told her. 'I'm just going down to change the lager barrel.'

I put on the light and went through a door at the back of the bar which opened immediately on to stone steps down to the cellar. The cellar had rows of metal barrels resting on racks against one breeze-block wall and plastic tubes leading up from the barrels through the ceiling to the bar above. Against another wall were dozens of cases of spirits.

The cellar was dank and dark but it had one curiosity. In one corner there was a self-contained cell with iron bars and a lock. But it was designed to keep people out rather than in. My father had it built years ago after mysterious thefts of wines and spirits from the cellar had threatened to wipe out his profits. It was too inconvenient to lock the cellar itself because members of staff were constantly going down to change the empty beer barrels, so he built the cell in the cellar to protect his most expensive drinks, particularly his champagne.

I didn't lock the cell myself because my staff, unlike his, could be trusted. Also, I had an aversion to cells, having languished in one in Germany under the tender ministrations of a Royal Air Force policeman called Edwin Catchpole.

Congratulating myself on my trustworthy staff, I transferred the pipes from the empty lager barrel to a full one and moved the empty barrel to be carried out to the yard later. Then I put a new full barrel on the rack ready to replace the one I had just connected. I hoped it would be replaced soon: there was a good profit in lager.

If genius is an infinite capacity for picking brains, I have it. Every week I make at least one furtive visit to a rival hostelry and submit their organization to the sort of scrutiny that would qualify me for a senior post in espionage. I sit in places where I am unknown and remember everything that I see. I discover the latest economies in catering and tomorrow's most fashionable drinks. I learn new solutions to old problems. I spot the trends at birth. When the drinking public began to switch from beer to lager the balance had already shifted in my cellar.

As I climbed the steps to the bar I decided to have a pint of it myself. However, the shock that awaited me as I entered the room sent me automatically for the Scotch. I had taken a step forward into the past and the whisky, which I rarely drank, disappeared quickly.

The party from Yorkshire had now taken up most of the space at the counter and they were gathered round the largest man among them. I recognized him instantly, even without the RAF uniform.

In a room full of people an animal will always stand out.

2

I disappeared from the bar in a matter of seconds and shut myself in my tiny office at the back of reception. Somewhere amid the accumulated debris of the years — letters, newspapers, magazines, maps — was an old photograph album, maintained religiously until I was twenty-one and never opened since. I found it eventually and turned to the final entries, a page of photographs taken one summer on an RAF camp in Germany.

The young airman who appeared in most of them, a slim man in his working blues with his LAC flashes on his arm and his short hair slicked down with Brylcreem, was a figure from another age. I took the pictures across to the mirror on the wall of my office and compared the man in the pictures with the man in the mirror. There must have been some resemblance but I couldn't see it. The face in the mirror was fatter, the hair was much longer and so thoroughly re-styled as to kill any likeness, and the eyes — no longer bright or curious or hopeful — seemed with twenty years' experience resting above them to have changed shape.

Catchpole wouldn't know me.

I took the album back to the desk and studied the pictures more closely. Surprisingly I could remember the names of all the airmen in them although we had not met since that oppressive summer.

One photograph stood out because there were no people in it. It was a picture of a dark single-storey building with wired-up windows and just one thick black door at the front. The building stood on its own in a lonely corner of the camp. The

24

name on its door in large white letters was clearly readable even in the tiny photograph taken, necessarily, from some distance: Field Punishment Detention Unit. As I put the album back into my desk some newspaper cuttings slipped from its pages. I tucked them into my wallet.

Back in the bar an immense and odoriferous lady magistrate, who would never be seen in a public house, was swilling back Bacardi like a pig at a trough. I watched approvingly: my prices weren't cheap. Next week, when she sobered up, she would be trying to deport parking offenders, but I wasn't coming up for a parking offence next week. A tall bespectacled Scotsman, with a clipped beard, whose face appeared frequently on my television set reporting the latest fiasco of the world of politics, was patriotically buying large quantities of his country's most famous export. 'Do you gamble, David?' somebody shouted at him. 'Does a fish swim?' he shouted back in a deep Edinburgh brogue. Next to him a man who looked like an ageing Clark Gable, and who had made a small fortune by patenting a paint roller which enabled you to paint the ceiling without half a pint of gloss dripping up your nose, was shouting for the hundredth time: 'Socialism never did anything for anybody.' The political reporter at his elbow preserved his professional impartiality by ignoring this.

Catchpole's group had established themselves at the bar and were talking in strong Yorkshire accents about golf. I used the mirror behind the drinks to see whether he was noticing me, but he wasn't. They interrupted the golf talk to howl for drinks.

I realized that Lisa had disappeared, probably to fetch sandwiches, and went up to them. A somewhat haggard young man, who had devoted more thought to his hair-style than seemed right in a well-adjusted human being, waved a five-pound note. His hair had been trimmed, waved and blow-dried so that he looked like a soap opera idol.

'An alligator sandwich and make it snappy,' said the would-be star.

This evidently passed for humour in his part of the world and so I laughed in the sycophantic manner occasionally required by my trade. What he actually wanted was six pints of brown and mild, the first time it had ever been ordered in the Bali. Catchpole spoke up, demanding a whisky chaser which he said he would pay for himself. I made a point of meeting his eyes: there was not a flicker of recognition. It occurred to me then that I was foolish to imagine that he could possibly remember me. He would have dealt with hundreds, maybe thousands, of airmen, none of them for very long.

But for me, of course, there was only one Catchpole.

I watched him guzzling his beer. Twenty years of self-indulgence had made no improvement to his appearance. His jawline was now barely visible beneath the layers of fat, and amid all the flesh that his head was burdened with his hard eyes stared out resentfully as if they, too, would soon vanish beneath the blubber.

Presently he levered himself off his stool and ambled off towards the lavatories. I seized the opportunity to discuss him.

'He's a big man,' I said to his group of friends.

'Catchpole?' said the soap opera star. 'He's a violent man, too.'

'Still?' I said, surprised.

'What do you mean "still"?' said one of the party.

I realized my mistake and corrected it.

'I mean at his age.'

'The last time Catchpole hit somebody outside a pub the police were looking for a hit-and-run driver,' said the soap opera star proudly. The others laughed raucously as they recalled this heart-warming episode.

When Lisa returned with some prawn sandwiches I sauntered out to the reception desk. Catchpole and his friends, I discovered, were from the Leeds area of Yorkshire and I remembered one of their number, a Gordon Hammerdale, writing to me from Garforth a few weeks earlier, inquiring about golf courses in the area and, on receiving my wild assurances on the subject, booking six single rooms for the holiday weekend. Edwin Catchpole, I noticed, had been given room seven. If brute strength was going to assist him on

26

his sporting break he would be holing his tee-shot from 600 yards.

He was back on his stool recounting the story of some small golfing triumph when I returned. The Yorkshire accent was so broad that it sounded like the effort of an actor with a poor talent for mimicry. His friends listened politely: it was apparent that the story was not new to them.

The latest arrival in the bar was a lonely young man who spent most of his time playing my fruit machine. To help him in this enterprise he had constructed a chart which recorded in what order the symbols appeared on each reel. He had shown it to me one night with great pride.

'Look at this,' he had said. 'There's only one grape on the first reel but four on the second, and there's only one pear on the middle reel but five on the first.'

I had stared at his artwork wonderingly. Anyone who thought that they were going to get rich from a fruit machine deserved to be let down lightly. But my sympathy was misplaced because the chart enabled him to hold the right symbols and to nudge in winning lines more often than anyone else.

He came across now and put two pounds of tokens on the counter. He wanted a lager.

'Still winning?' I asked.

'Candy from babies,' he said. 'Have a drink yourself.'

'Ever thought of taking up beautiful women?' I asked. 'They're a sort of fruit machine substitute.'

'If I don't have my glasses on I don't spot them,' he said. 'And if I put them on they don't fancy me.'

'A combination of myopia and vanity that seems to add up to celibacy,' I said.

The fruit machine man considered this. 'I get my kicks from jackpots,' he said.

'You are clearly in the grip of a terrible addiction,' I told him. I didn't mind telling him: it was my money that he was winning. He gathered up his drink and the tokens that were left and wandered back to the machine. Soon the clatter of another win could be heard across the room.

The bar was crowded now with people unwinding for the holiday weekend, most of them clutching a drink and a cigarette — stimulant in one hand, sedative in the other. The television reporter, discovering the aphrodisiac effect of fame, was now in danger of being seduced by the lady magistrate; the Clark Gable figure was telling a man I hadn't seen before that Socialism had never done anything for anybody; a loud young car salesman, who fancied himself sartorially and was known as the immaculate misconception, was looking for somewhere to plant his evil seed so that the world would eventually be burdened with his replacement; a remarkably taciturn man from the gas board was buying his party all the drinks, generosity being the last resort of the inarticulate; and a man who had drunk three light ales had put on a fez.

The low-pitched buzz of a dozen conversations drifted across the smoky room and although most of them were not worth the effort I had become a practised eavesdropper. Modish cant by the bucketful was reaching me now from some youngsters standing a few yards away, and to one side of them a mixed group of forty-year-olds were drowning in a sea of economic clichés, replete with Pandora's Boxes full of Trojan Horses.

But the sound that I was hearing best tonight was the humourless blare of Edwin Catchpole which was now, slurred with the drink, enlightening its captive audience with a long and rambling story about its owner's attempt to reproduce himself on a golf course in Northumberland.

His voice revived unpleasant memories and I drifted down the counter to my friends.

Mrs Stapleton was demanding evidence of Adam's literary talent, and reluctantly he pulled some sheets of paper from the back pocket of his jeans.

'This is the short story I wrote today,' he said.

'Read it,' commanded Mrs Stapleton.

Adam smoothed a piece of paper on one knee.

'The doorbell rang,' he read. 'Do you like that start? I wondered whether to have "the telephone rang" but I

28

thought the physical presence of a visitor would be more effective.'

'How about the campanologist rang?' suggested Mrs Stapleton.

Adam ignored her and continued to read. 'Gavin came into the room in a rush and pushed something into Mary's hand. It was mail — and urgent.'

'Male and urgent?' said Mrs Stapleton. 'The dirty little sod.'

'The telegram boy stood shivering at the door, waiting to see if there was a reply.'

'We don't have telegram boys any more, do we?' said Mrs Stapleton. 'What year does this take place?'

Adam scowled at her. 'I think I'll give up writing,' he said.

'It sounds like the greatest blow to literature since Vesuvius killed Pliny the Elder,' said Mrs Stapleton. 'I should quit while you're behind.'

Adam folded the story up and returned it to his pocket. 'One door shuts and another door slams,' he said.

Mrs Stapleton patted him on the shoulder. Her other hand was clutching an empty glass, a sight which always disturbed me.

'Fill 'em up,' she said, 'and get the writer one, too. I always know when I've drunk too much — I start buying people drinks.'

Adam emptied his glass. 'Your generosity underwhelms me, madam, but your literary criticism hurts.'

'If you would abandon your pretentious distaste for money I think you would do very well elsewhere,' said Mrs Stapleton briskly. 'What you need is get-up-and-go.'

'I'm more your sit-down-and-stay.'

'The outcome is no income,' declared Mrs Stapleton, cradling her newly filled gin. 'Frank Winfield Woolworth borrowed two hundred dollars from his landlady to open a shop.'

'I borrowed fifty pounds from my landlady to buy a hundredweight of used gym shoes.'

'I think I'm beginning to see the scope of the problem,'

said Mrs Stapleton. 'Marriage is the only thing that will save you — the road to success is filled with women pushing their men along.'

'Success? I'll probably wind up in a cave living on berries and goat's milk.'

'Spoken like a true idiot. Why don't you get a girl? I must say that your talent for finding them is less than talismanic.'

Adam drank from his mug and belched mildly.

'Can I press you to a tart, Vicar?' Mrs Stapleton chortled. 'Of course, your *louche* behaviour may be a stumbling-block in the quest for love. I reckon the last time you were in bed with a woman was when you were born.'

'About then,' said Adam, nodding. 'What a waste! Do you realize that a hundred thousand people in this country are probably making love at this very moment?'

'And fifty thousand of them are having orgasms.'

Adam raised his hand defensively. 'We don't want any of that feminist stuff in here. Why isn't there a masculist movement, anyway?'

'Because,' said Mrs Stapleton, 'throughout history women have been used, abused and confused by male chauvinists like you and Martin. Getting you two buggers to marry is like trying to persuade pandas to mate.'

I resisted the temptation to contradict this: I wasn't going to expose my romantic plans to the withering crossfire of the Bali.

'You can always tell the married couples in here, Alice,' I said. 'They're the ones who never smile at each other.'

She wheeled round on her stool to face me. 'What happened to that nubile soubrette you had staying here a few weeks ago, anyway? What was her name?'

'Laurel. As a matter of fact she is coming down on Sunday for a few days.'

'Good,' said Mrs Stapleton. 'I hope you'll bear my wishes in mind.'

'I always bear your wishes in mind,' I said. 'You are my most valued customer.'

'I should think so, too,' she said. 'Now what about tomorrow's racing? Have you any good tips for me?'

'You ask me that every week,' I said. 'But you never back my selections.'

'Quite so,' she replied. 'But knowing which horses you fancy helps me to make up my mind.'

She was suddenly distracted by Catchpole shouting for drinks.

'I don't like that man,' she said, and placed a finger across the bridge of her nose. 'His face from here down wobbles.'

I went down the bar to serve him, Lisa having vanished again, and then spent some time watching him and his group.

So by the time I managed to close the bar it was a former RAF policeman who filled my thoughts instead of the lady who was intended to dominate my thinking this weekend.

Trips down memory lane have always seemed to me to be an unprofitable pastime, but that night in bed, anxious to recapture the last repellent detail of Catchpole's personality, I allowed myself the doubtful pleasure of recollection.

3

Forty years ago — several millennia late by the evolutionary clock — a creature hauled himself from the primeval swamps, balanced unsteadily on his hind legs and pronounced himself a man. His name was Edwin Catchpole and he was now installed in room seven. I might be a little harsh about his origins. Perhaps he sprang from a long line of human beings, but his behaviour leads me to believe otherwise.

The moment we met he knocked me twenty feet down a stone corridor with a blow to the side of the head that I had not been expecting. Had I known that this was how he greeted people I should have braced myself for the introduction, but as he then weighed eighteen stone I would still have travelled involuntarily some distance down the corridor, say nineteen feet. The circumstances of our meeting were, like most of my life up till then, not of my choosing.

A new rebellious generation has flowered since that hot and memorable summer. In the schools a new educational philosophy has shifted the emphasis from coercion to co-operation, and in the home apathetic parents call themselves libertarian. Rising teenagers, with the highest illiteracy rate for years, vandalize phone kiosks, frighten old ladies, mug strangers and kick heads as casually as their fathers once punched noses.

I missed all this fun by some years. And no sooner had I escaped from the oppressive regime of an uncompromising boys' school than I was despatched to Germany for two years' National Service in the Royal Air Force.

I counted the days — the minutes flew like hours — and with 549 days and seventeen hours done I believed that I

32

could see the light at the end of the tunnel. The light, however, was an approaching train.

I have always believed in making money where you can — a shortage of it is at the root of most of the world's problems — and as I left the camp one evening with my usual supply of a thousand cigarettes I was stopped by a new RAF policeman, clearly ambitious to succeed in his miserable calling.

'Bartering cigarettes is a heinous crime, airman,' he said. 'Step inside this guardroom.' I have always remembered his use of the word heinous: national servicemen were an unpredictable bunch.

Corporal Edwin Catchpole, despite his weight, was then about twenty-two. He was six feet three but the face that topped this mountain was a child's. It was flabby and white with sleepy eyes and a baby's mouth. It didn't look as if it had yet been introduced to the razor blade.

'Name, scum?' said this genetic freak when I met him the following day, two weeks in the Field Punishment Detention Unit being the going rate for bartering cigarettes. It was when I called him corporal instead of staff that he hit me for the first time.

The detention unit was L-shaped and consisted of two long corridors with cells on either side; the outside, oblong shape of the unit was completed by the punishment yard. Through the door that led into the yard, I could see a tall man in a brown denim boiler suit running very quickly on the spot while holding an eight-foot form at arm's length above his head. Every so often torrents of water hit him in the face, thrown, presumably, from unseen buckets round the corner.

Along the corridor two other men in denims were leaning against cell doors. They were facing the doors with their feet a yard or more away, and they were taking their weight on the middle fingers of each hand.

'Don't move,' Catchpole shouted down to them. 'That's the Russian treatment,' he told me. 'You'll enjoy that.'

In the punishment yard the man who had been running

had collapsed. Two RAF policemen were throwing buckets of water over him.

'A most interesting place you've got ...' I started to say, and came round, seconds later, on the cold tiles of the corridor.

A few feet from where I lay was a manhole. A voice, low and furious, drifted up from it: 'Let me out, you bastards.'

They dragged me to my feet and locked me in a cell. There was nothing in it except a wooden board and a grey blanket. I sat down and felt the back of my head, wondering what they had hit me with. There was blood on my fingers. For a few moments I considered flattening the next policeman that I saw but when I stood up I was dizzy and stumbled across the stone floor to lean against the wall. The door opened and a policeman I hadn't seen before threw in the brown denim boiler suit uniform.

'Get that on, pants, boots, nothing else,' he said. 'Bring the rest out when you have changed.'

They exchanged my uniform for a bucket of water and a scrubbing brush.

'Scrub that cell, scum,' Catchpole said. I returned to my cell to scrub the floor, wondering if anybody had ever died in here. Catchpole followed me in, kicked the bucket of water over, smiled and went out.

At dinner that evening I met my fellow-prisoners. There were eight of them: the unit had more staff than customers. We sat in a small room off one of the corridors eating food that had been brought over from the airmen's mess. We ate it with a spoon; no prisoner was going to be trusted with anything as lethal as a knife or fork.

No one spoke and we ate in silence so I never did find out what offences my colleagues had committed. Three policemen supervised the meal, and when it was finished one of them half filled a mug with syrup and then added tea.

'Drink this, Doyle,' he said to one of the airmen. A pale, wild-eyed boy of about eighteen stood up and took the mug. 'Doyle hasn't moved very quickly today, have you, Doyle?' he said.

34

Doyle drank from the mug, slowly at first and then quickly to get it over with. While he drank the policeman filled another one in the same way. He handed it to Doyle, who looked at it and then drank it, but not as quickly as he had the first one. A third one followed and then a fourth, which Doyle couldn't finish.

Catchpole came in, smiling. 'Whose turn is it to puke tonight?' he said.

'Doyle's,' said the policeman who had been filling the mug.

'Last one in the punishment yard scrubs the corridor,' said Catchpole. A wild rush for the door left me standing; even Doyle beat me to it.

Outside we were lined up against a wall like men waiting for the firing-squad. Catchpole sauntered out after us. 'Doyle, two paces forward, running on the spot — begin!'

Doyle was sick very quickly but was not allowed to stop running. If he slowed Catchpole hit him across the shoulders with a rifle. He jogged on, vomiting intermittently down his chest.

At half-past five in the morning a dustbin was hurled from one end of the corridor to the other. Prisoners were advised to be up and dressed before the echo faded. I didn't know this on my first morning. I had been up until midnight scrubbing the corridors, a reward for reaching the punishment yard last, and I heard the key in the door as I eased myself up on one elbow. It was surprising how well you could sleep on a wooden board if you were tired enough. The scrubbing had used muscles that had seldom been called on and my back and the backs of my legs ached. Catchpole burst into the cell and dragged me up by my hair.

'You should have done half an hour's work by now,' he said, hitting me, open handed, across the face. 'Get dressed, scum. Get a bucket. Get scrubbing this pig sty cell.'

From the bathroom along the corridor there came the sound of a man screaming. Outside in the yard others were already running.

I dressed quickly and went out to find a bucket. In the

bathroom, where the water was, three policemen had fixed a noose from the pipes across the ceiling and tied it round one of the airmen's necks. He was standing on a chair with his hands tied behind his back.

'Stop the screaming,' said one of the policemen. 'We're only going to hang you. We'll say it was suicide, see?'

The airman on the chair had the fixed stare of a man already dead. He seemed to have lost the ability to scream now and had gone quiet.

A policeman drew his leg back, as if to kick the chair away.

I spoke. 'These pigs won't kill you,' I told him. 'They'd have to kill all of us . . .'

Whatever else I was planning to say remained unsaid as all three policemen fell on me, hitting out with boots and fists.

'Put him in the manhole,' one of them shouted. 'Cool him off.'

I blacked out then from some unseen blow and came round in a very small, dark space, with the sound of men running up and down the corridor above my head. Swelling seemed to have closed one eye and my ribs ached in different places, but it was peaceful sitting alone in the dark and I made myself as comfortable as I could and tried to sleep. Later I wondered whether I had slept — it was difficult to tell — but a long time after that I knew that I had because of a vivid dream about a suicide from a high building: a man had plunged head first from the roof of an office and landed only feet from where I stood. I waited in the dark and tried to guess the time. Hunger came and went. Occasionally water dripped on my head as the corridor above was scrubbed yet again.

Finally I heard them wrestling with the manhole cover and suddenly light poured in. Two policemen pulled me out but, once in the corridor, I had to lean against a wall to stay upright. The clock on the wall by the front door said six o'clock: I had been in the manhole for exactly twelve hours.

Once a week a padre visited the unit. He was an Air Force officer who wore his disparate hats with great virtuosity.

The prisoners paraded in the yard and he went from one to the next asking if they had any complaints. The men he was talking to had black eyes, cut faces, swollen lips and other bumps and lumps, but he didn't seem to notice. I wondered whether he had once done missionary work in Africa and imagined that these cicatrices indicated each man's region of origin.

'What do you think?' I asked sullenly when the padre reached me with his usual question.

'Jolly good,' he said nervously and moved on. My devout atheism dates from this brief conversation, which Catchpole, a yard or two behind, overheard.

'Your turn to be sick tonight,' he whispered.

Days passed painfully. New prisoners arrived and deflected some of the staff's venom. One, a huge man who was reputed to have beaten up two sergeants, opening one of their faces with a tin helmet, received strangely preferential treatment. Another, who tried to cut his wrist with a knife he had found in the canteen, was taken away in the middle of the night to station sick quarters. I never talked to anybody. Conversation was impossible and even an exchange of winks was punished.

In my last few days I was left alone. The reason was obvious: they wanted the visible injuries to fade. I did what I had to do and kept my mouth shut. My eye was still discoloured but the swelling had gone. I felt unusually fit after the non-stop exercise, which in the early days had buckled me, and I began to feel good.

With two days to go my confidence spilled over.

Catchpole, at a loose end, strolled into my cell while I was scrubbing the floor. Routinely, he kicked the bucket over and watched satisfied as the tides of dirty water covered the whole floor.

'Mop it up, scum. Get moving. You're not out yet.'

I stood up and stared into his eyes, curious finally about what was going on in this man's head. Catchpole stared back, unused to something which in this building surpassed insolence and almost amounted to aggression.

'This isn't going to last for ever,' I said, bracing myself already for the bruises that were to come. 'One day we will meet again.'

'We will?' Catchpole said, the smile returning slowly.

'I'll make sure of it.'

Catchpole looked at me incredulously. It was probably the longest speech that any prisoner had ever made. He said something — 'sounds like a threat' was a phrase that I heard — and jammed his knee upwards into my groin. As I doubled forward in pain, Catchpole smiled and brought the knee up again into my face.

And now he was in room seven!

Part Two

Saturday

4

I was not going to allow the unwelcome arrival of Edwin Catchpole to distract me from the weekend's romantic climax: a man doesn't become engaged to marry every day.

I have done my share of belittling the marriage institution, particularly with the help of a few drinks, but after a certain age a man alone is as natural as a three-legged dog. This is not a view that I have expressed publicly: it would contradict too much of what has gone before. Until the first of last month — a mere eight weeks ago — I was more likely to suggest that if a permanent relationship between a man and a woman had not become a sort of human tradition, it would never occur to the majority of men to try it.

Adam was my uncertain ally in this misogynists' *pas de deux*. 'A bachelor is a person who never makes the same mistake once', was his favourite saying, but I had seen the wistful look in his eyes.

Mrs Stapleton was my doughty opponent. She was fond of describing me as a male chauvinist, whatever that is (chauvinism meant a kind of aggressive patriotism when I went to school), but she misunderstood me. I don't want to relegate women to a second-class position; I want them to stop trying to do it to men. I have listened amazed as men lied about their presence in my bar to avoid strife at home. A domineering wife, ruling the house with angry silences, is no less cruel than a violent husband. The sex war has always been real to me — it isn't the abstract idea of some trendy journalists. It's fought in my bar every day.

All of which left me somewhat abashed at the beginning of

41

last month when I had to consider the possibility that I had fallen in love.

It is not a condition that is easily diagnosed by a doctor or even by the suspected victim, but something happened. It didn't result in a loss of appetite or concentration or sleep — that triple bereavement which women's magazines like to imagine is the natural concomitant of sudden passion — but I did start to behave a little oddly. I not only went out of my way to find the lady, I went out of my way to please her. On one occasion, apparently, I mentioned marriage.

This uncharacteristic behaviour was brought on by a girl who was not even pretty; the look in her eyes, which promised fun and sin in equal quantities, the sound of her voice, which was a kind of low-pitched purr, and her lively, lovely unconventional personality were far more lethal than the pretty faces that I had mistakenly sought before.

She arrived in a cloud of dust on a Saturday afternoon. The dust was caused by her taxi, which skidded to a halt on the hotel's gravel forecourt. She jumped out, paid the taxi and marched up to my reception desk with blue matching suitcases in each hand.

She wanted a room for a week.

'Single?' I said.

She held up a ring-less left hand.

I smiled. 'I meant the room.'

'With a table,' she said. 'I have work to do.'

I pushed the register towards her more out of curiosity than duty and watched her sign her name: L. Sherman. She was a short girl with auburn hair and a fine shape. Her nose was too big but her eyes sparkled and her mouth was set permanently at a half smile. She affected me from the very beginning.

'L for Laurel,' she said. 'Are you the porter?'

'More or less,' I replied, picking up her cases. I led her up the stairs and along one of the corridors to a favourite room overlooking the river. The delicate fragrance of polish hung lightly in the air — I didn't want the Bali to smell like one of those architectural monstrosities in foreign holiday resorts where the heavy stench of the hotel's cheap polish lingers in your nostrils even when you are lying on a windy beach.

I placed the cases by her bed and saw tuppence lying on the thick blue carpet.

'Is that my tip?' I asked.

'I don't know,' she said, staring at me. 'What does your tip look like?'

I hurried from the room. At opening time she came into the bar.

'Who owns this dump?' she asked.

'I do,' I told her.

'Whoops!' she said, putting her hand over her mouth. 'Can I buy you a drink?'

'You mean "may I," ' I said, anxious now to shuffle off my hall porter's persona.

'Do I? In Scotland it's "will I." Anyway, shall I?'

She bought me a sherry and insisted on clinking glasses.

'Up yours,' she said, laughing loudly. She was wearing a white dress in fine cotton with camisole top and wrapover skirt. She had snakeskin sandals and a snakeskin clutch bag.

'Laurel Sherman,' I said. 'You look like someone who keeps moving.'

She dived into the bag which she had dropped on the floor and came up holding her passport.

'Never go anywhere without it,' she said.

I seldom bothered to start conversations, having had my share of chatty but crepuscular barmen, barbers and taxi drivers. I let others choose the subject — I am an adroit verbal counter-puncher — but this sublime elf had provoked my curiosity.

'What does it say alongside occupation?' I asked.

She looked — there had obviously been some career changes — and announced: 'Astrologer. Do you know anything about it?'

'I know that Sirius, the dog star, is one of our nearest stellar neighbours and is hotter than the sun.'

'That's astronomy, you pratt! I write horoscopes.' She laughed loudly again. 'I write your stars for six different magazines and I've come down here to get a few months ahead so I can take time off. I hope my typewriter won't keep you awake.'

'I'm Pisces,' I said. 'How do things look?'

'Single Pisces or married Pisces?'

'Single Pisces.'

'They look pretty good.'

She sipped her sherry thoughtfully.

'If you're the hall porter, the barman and the owner, isn't it time you got into the kitchen to cook the dinner? The hotels I usually stay in employ what they call staff.'

'The chef is preparing dinner,' I told her. 'The barmaid doesn't start until seven-thirty.'

'I can see that over-manning isn't a problem at the Bali Hotel.'

'I believe that you'll find the service satisfactory, though,' I told her. 'If you want anything, just shout.'

'I'll remember that.'

Her meaning was clear enough and I smiled at her. I have made love to several guests at the Bali — it is one of the perks that I had anticipated when I moved in. Making love to women I hardly know is more enjoyable than sleeping with an old friend. A woman's sex appeal seems to fade for me in direct proportion to the amount of time that I have known her.

She returned to the bar after dinner. A pink bow had appeared in her hair. She walked over to the french windows and went out on to the patio. When our climate allowed it, customers liked to drink there seated under green and white parasols, watching the ducks on the river. There were several there now.

I followed her to the door.

'Would you like me to bring a drink out to you?' I asked. She was already heading for preferential treatment.

'It's beautiful, isn't it?' she said. 'You can almost hear the silence. I've always fancied living in the country. I'm a city girl myself.'

'Which city?'

'Place called London.' She turned round. 'No, I'll come in and drink with you. Dinner was excellent, by the way.' She jumped on to a high stool at the bar. 'Okay, bring on the alcohol.'

'Alcohol?'

'It's a carbo-hydrate, usually made from grain.'

'I meant what variety?'

'Cloberg,' she said. 'Chilled.'

When I had poured her wine, Lisa appeared and so I slipped round to the other side to join the new guest.

'It's a nice place,' she said, looking round. 'I usually drink in one of those plastic bars where it's not even real plastic.'

'I hope you enjoy your visit,' I said. 'What do the stars predict?'

'Undiluted pleasure. I wrote it myself.'

'You believe in that stuff?'

'Of course not. I believe in undiluted pleasure though. What's your name?'

'Martin Lomax.'

'And you're not married. In ancient Greece they used to arrest bachelors of thirty. You are over thirty, I take it?'

'I'm thirty-eight.'

'That's quite old, isn't it?'

'Senile. Most of our top sportsmen weren't even born when I was their age.'

'You're quite right to be single, though,' she said. 'That with my body I thee honour stuff always struck me as rather vain.'

She drank some wine and stared at me over the rim of her glass. I realized with a shock that she wanted to go to bed with me.

If I have a fault it is that I am too modest.

The discovery threw me a little and I forgot what I was going to say next. There was a long silence, a rare event in the Bali's bar.

'The conversation flowed like Vaseline,' said my cheerful companion.

'Tell me about yourself,' I said feebly. What I wanted to know about was her lovelife. Attractive girls did not reach her age, which I judged to be the mid-twenties, without some romantic bruising.

45

'I went to Cambridge,' she said. 'The cream of today, the cheese of tomorrow.'

'And now you're an astrologer?'

'We didn't all end up at the BBC.'

On the other side of the bar the clatter of a jackpot marked up another triumph for the fruit machine man. When the noise subsided, Laurel said, 'Show me your hotel.'

We finished our drinks and went upstairs: it would have been a fatally naïve mistake to show her the kitchen. We went past her room and along the corridor to the stairs that led up to my untidy flat. Fortunately I had made the large double bed in the centre of my bedroom and the place looked less squalid than usual. Laurel sat on the bed as if testing its springs.

'Your place or mine?' I said.

'Oh, I think yours. Sit down here, Martin. What a pleasant life you must lead down here in the country. The lazy days and the wicked nights.'

I sat next to her on the bed. 'And the busy days and the celibate nights.'

'How sad. Shall I give you the dance of the seven bathroom towels?'

'I'd certainly like to take your clothes off.'

'But unfortunately you haven't got them on.'

I kissed her and she stopped fooling then. Her clothes seemed to disappear before my eyes. I sometimes think that my generation has been spoilt by pin-up magazines: the busty perfection of the gatefold girl is difficult to match. But Laurel looked as if she had stepped straight out of its pages.

We lay and talked and made love and laughed.

'We've only known each other two or three hours,' she said.

'I'm afraid that doesn't beat any records round here,' I said.

'What is your record?'

'Thirty-five minutes.'

She lay on her back, her hands behind her head, and said, ' "The duke returned early from the wars and pleasured me twice in his top boots." That's my favourite sentence in all literature.'

My thirty-five-minute record, a source of considerable pride, was clearly of no interest to her.

'Years ago when I was young . . .' I began.

'When body-snatchers filched cadavers?'

'Before that.'

'When men traded pelts?'

'Round about then. A left breast used to last three hours. Now you have to make love to a girl six times before she will look at your etchings.'

'I think that's progress, don't you?' said Laurel, laying an arm across my chest. 'Her not bothering about your etchings?'

For the rest of that week I had a lurking feeling that I was on trial, but what standards I was supposed to attain were never revealed. I also had a suspicion that there was at least one other man in Laurel's life, but no information on that subject was vouchsafed either. When I made remarks which suggested implicitly that our relationship was not going to be confined to this wild and wonderful week, she remained delightfully non-committal. She revealed a formidable talent for talking a lot and promising nothing.

She spent some time in her room, foreseeing excitement, love, travel and glamour for the horoscope-reading millions, but there was never a hint that she could see any of these ingredients in my own misty future. She became a hit at the bar with her cheerfulness and her wisecracks, and at night she shared my bed, where her behaviour suggested that if the world was going to separate us it would need a water-cannon to do it.

But in the cooler light of day I knew that somebody or something was pulling on the other end of the rope.

The second half of her stay was packed with a series of small disasters. I took her to a theatre that always had spare seats and it had sold out; so we went to a night-club, but it was closed. Laurel didn't make much of this but I could sense the black marks being entered in some ledger. I rushed her to the sea and it rained without a break.

But the biggest humiliation was still to come.

With two days to go her departure hung over me like a

sickness. I could see her dropping out of my life as suddenly as she had appeared. I invited her to stay on but she was unresponsive. I offered free accommodation indefinitely but she shook her head. I was put in my place without her having to say it: I had been a temporary diversion.

I was about to play my last card — the offer of a partnership of her choosing — when something else happened instead. I found her on the patio one evening studying a colour feature in one of her magazines on bull-fighting. It seemed to fascinate her.

'I've been groped by a Balkan high-jumper in Belgrade. I've been touched up in the funiculaire at the Sacré Coeur, and I've come third in a camel race at Rabat but, oddly enough, I have never seen a bull-fight,' said my favourite astrologer.

You don't have to throw a line to a drowning man twice.

The following morning we were on a plane to Bilbao, *en route*, as they say in Spain, for the week-long fiesta of San Fermin in Pamplona. As we swept in low over the Bay of Biscay I sat back congratulating myself on my enterprise, my quick thinking — my generosity. I wasn't to know that the relationship was already doomed by the displeasure of a malign deity somewhere.

Within half an hour of landing we had hired a Seat car and were driving across northern Spain in the sun while I gave my standard lecture on the bull-fight. We arrived in Pamplona late in the afternoon.

The ancient city was full of people in red berets and red scarves dancing through the tiny streets to drums, halting the traffic and creating an atmosphere of wild gaiety. Tired-looking youngsters from all over the world put down their sleeping-bags to join in the fun.

We queued for three hours to get tickets for that evening's bull-fight, but my bad luck held and they sold out just before we reached the window.

'There's always tomorrow and the next day and the next,' I said. 'It goes on for a week.'

We were sitting at the beer tables in the Avenida de Roncesvalles opposite the bull-ring, looking at the ladies with flowers in their hair and watching small girls begging with plastic cups. From the windows of a building on a corner, nuns looked down bleakly at the drunken revelry.

'Well,' said Laurel, 'I hope they don't sell out of tickets tomorrow.'

We walked down the Estafeta, the narrow street in the old part of the city that the bulls came running through every morning on their way to the bull-ring. The crowds ran ahead of them then, risking injury or death, and every morning a dozen or more were taken off to the hospital where they would spend the rest of the fiesta. I was looking forward to watching the running of the bulls, but from the safe side of the wooden barriers that were erected for one week every year to guide the bulls from their corral to the ring.

The hotels were full and we had to drive several miles out of Pamplona into the hills to find a hostel for the night.

When we returned in the morning the fiesta was over.

The red berets and red scarves had disappeared, the crowds were silent and tense and armed police with grey wagons stood scowling on every corner.

There had been a riot in the bull-ring the previous evening, we learned, and it had carried on afterwards in the streets. A student, a member of the Liga Komunista Iraultzailea, had been shot dead, and the posters were already going up condemning police repression. One showed the dead student with a bullet-hole in the middle of his forehead. He looked very young.

The town itself looked as if a bomb had hit it. The wooden barriers, used for running the bulls, had been chopped to matchwood, the windows in all the government buildings had been smashed and cars had been overturned and burnt. The internal wires were all that was left of their tyres. The bars were shut.

'This is a fiesta?' said Laurel.

'This was a fiesta,' I said.

'It's a long way to come not to see a bull-fight.'

I felt like an idiot.

'We'll find another,' I promised.

I bought a map of Navarre and studied it in the car. We had a long, slow lunch and then drove north. There had been a quarter of a million people in Pamplona and they were all leaving at once; a town full of armed policemen was bad for tourism. The roads out were lined two or three deep with hitch-hikers.

It was that part of the country where dry Spain meets green Spain, and as we drove over the hills to San Sebastian the scenery became progressively more French.

'Supposing there is no bull-ring in San Sebastian?' said Laurel.

'Of course there's a bull-ring,' I said. 'All the big towns have one.'

There is no bull-ring in San Sebastian.

Paradoxically this seemed to cheer Laurel up: certain suspicions about the quality of her companion were being confirmed. She smiled but said nothing.

I left the car and had a long talk with a policeman. He seemed surprised that anyone should expect a *plaza de toros* in San Sebastian. However, there was one up the coast in Fuenterrabia.

We drove on in the evening sunshine, but time was against us. Fuenterrabia was one of the most beautiful towns that I had seen. The tall, clean, old houses were brightly painted and covered with flowers. Many had bars which ran straight through the building to the road at the back. Everywhere people sat at tables sipping drinks in the cheerful streets, and across the harbour you could see the French coast.

However, we did not find a bull-ring. Even if there was one there we arrived too late to start looking. We sat in the Calle de San Pedro and ate stuffed peppers and shrimps.

Laurel hardly spoke and I was a long way short of chatty myself. It was the only time that I — or, quite conceivably, anybody else — had failed three times in one day to see a bull-fight.

On Saturday afternoons at the Bali I retired to my eyrie and allowed my Toshiba television and the weekly magazines to compete for my attention. It was a strangely quiet day, at least until the evening revellers appeared. But today I had the pleasure of a letter from Laurel, her first communication since Pamplona, which had arrived two days earlier and which I had now read fourteen times with increasing admiration.

It lay at the side of my bed now like a much-prized trophy.

I would like to say that the walls of my bedroom boast a harbour scene from Turner or a French landscape from Monet but, apart from a six-foot map of the world, the only illustration is a poster of Debbie Harry, finger on lips and BAD written across the chest of her black sweater. Presumably unconnected with this fantasy, but lying nearby, is a dusty and discarded Bullworker. I don't seem to have the energy of a year ago but who has? I have lost interest in keeping fit, but tell myself, wittily, that I get enough exercise walking at the funerals of my athletic friends.

I pushed a knob on the television and was granted immediate access to the glitterati of sport. I am not a great television fan but remain endlessly fascinated by the cameraman's penchant for lingering on hawking footballers, ball-scratching cricketers and thoughtful politicians absently involved in detailed nostril tours. This inadvertent stuff has twice the entertainment value of the narcoleptic chat show or the flawless, pre-recorded extravaganza.

On to the screen now came a gabbled report from our man in the studio on the weekend's sporting highlights. There was a Test match at the Oval, Walker Cup golf at Monterey and racing drivers were warming up for the Dutch Grand Prix at Zandvoort. The football season had opened with a £1,000-a-week 'star' being sent off for spitting.

It was either this or a film about 'an overwhelming passion that even nature could not destroy', and eventually I turned off my one-eyed companion and reached for the magazines. The one that I picked up was not the serious weekly fare that I used to exercise my mind at weekends, but a more popular publication that carried Laurel's horoscope and had been left by her the previous month. Men Fake Orgasms Too! it announced on the cover.

Inside I read:

ARE YOU A SUPERSTUD?
Try our Fun Quiz!
1 Afterwards, does she say:
  (a) Christ almighty
  (b) Thank you
  (c) Was that it?
Score A–2; B–1; C–0

It looked like another examination that I would probably fail and I put it to one side and found an interesting article about the bug revolution. Bugs can now be used to mine zinc, copper and uranium! In Brazil bug-produced alcohol will be fuelling most of the nation's cars by the end of the century! Bugs can make vaccines for flu, hepatitis and foot and mouth disease! Biologists are now able to make bugs to order and turn them into living factories!

Bugs were going to inherit the earth. It came as no surprise to me. I tried the radio news and caught a gem: the holiday weekend had begun with long waits at airports because of industrial action by baggage handlers. The English channel was more oil than water after a tanker collision. Rail fares were going up in the autumn. The weather forecast, predictably for a summer bank holiday, was torrential rain.

But the truth was that my mind was reluctant to grapple with the ephemeral excitements of radio and television. The malevolent presence in room seven was proving too intrusive.

I hadn't seen Edwin Catchpole all day. His party had taken an early breakfast, I was told by Judy, and headed for the golf course. No doubt an extended stay at the nineteenth hole would make them boisterous company this evening, if they chose to spend it at the hotel.

It seemed to me, lying on my bed, that Corporal Catchpole hadn't been delivered into the professional care of the Bali Hotel by accident. There were too many others he could have chosen. A bored fate was clearly inviting me to level the score.

For a long time I wondered what I could possibly do that would prove hurtful to him. Hotel owners did not, traditionally, knock their customers about, and even if they did they would make an exception for this surly giant. I tried to imagine a more subtle method of letting Mr Catchpole know that not everybody loved him. I could make him sick for a week but that would reflect badly on the Bali's kitchens. I could throw him out of the hotel on some dreamed-up grounds but would only lose the money that his drunken group were going to spend somewhere. I could ensure, in various ways, that he had a sleepless weekend but, ensuring it, I would have one too. I could easily arrange a broken leg or other injury with a mishap in the car park, but by the time the insurance man had done his duty it would probably hurt me more than him.

It was unthinkable that he should enjoy a carefree, happy weekend in my hotel — I owed it to myself to see that he didn't. But after half an hour the only acceptable reprisal I could envisage involved his losing large sums of money to me, perhaps with a bet. Even this idea didn't bear much examination. He probably didn't have large sums of money, and certainly not with him. Anyway, how could I be sure that he gambled?

I decided to thrust Edwin Catchpole from my thoughts for the time being and concentrate on more pleasant matters. The fifteenth reading of Laurel's letter was long overdue:

Get out the rolled reindeer on toast and the parfait of cloudberry — something lovely this way comes. My dogooding flatmate Mary Ann had gone down to the Thames to liven up the Seamen's Mission (or the missionary's semen) and my new paperback on the vicissitudes of a Parsi family in Lahore has lost my attention for the tenth time in ten pages. So I got to thumbing introspectively through my diary and can announce, without fear of contraceptive, that next weekend is called the Late Summer Holiday weekend. Where better to spend it, I thought, than at Martin's *gasthof*? Some enchanted evenings at the Bali! I ignore the fact that you have ignored me since the fiesta/fiasco and foist myself quite shamelessly upon you.

I yearn for the sight of a tree. In this man's city of concrete and dog's turds you can easily forget what the real world looks like. I wish to enjoy the smell of new-mown grass and will cut your lawns specially to create it. I want to inhale a lungful of air without coughing. I crave peace. The most deafening sound that I shall allow to disturb my tranquillity will be a sparrow farting in the next meadow but one.

Shall I visit your pastoral paradise? Speak now or forever hold your penis.

I have, you will be amazed to learn, lately severed all relationships with the opposite sex, having gone through an experimental phase in which I allowed myself to be wooed exclusively by foreigners. From Mustapha P. Quick, the incontinent Arab, I learned how to lose at roulette, and from a Sudanese potter in Cricklewood I learned how to potter about. There was a rather sexist Spaniard, who tried to make up in generosity for what he lacked in charm, and a very serious American, built like a bus shelter, who was teaching himself Russian so that he could read Dostoevsky in the original. It was to this last one that I was attached when we met, which made my position somewhat ambivalent. But that's all behind me now, as the chap with piles said, and to all intense and porpoises the world is my lobster. As we girls without piles say, you gotta kiss a lot of frogs before you find a prince.

When are you going to take me to see the Rift Valley, the Great Barrier Reef, the Himalayas or the Grand Canyon? America is a wonderful country. Few chaps arrived there on a boat not so long ago — now they've got electricity, sewage, the lot. Just because we couldn't find a bull-fight in Spain it doesn't mean that we would miss the Empire State Building in Manhattan. We could get lucky. When I was young I dreamed of travelling there dangerously and becoming a tabloid heroine. Girl Crosses Atlantic On Upturned Toilet Seat Fighting Off Sharks With Granny's Brolly.

I am sorry to waffle on in this way. I suddenly feel very

happy at the thought of seeing you. Life is a high-jump but I can't decide whether I'm a straddler or a flopper. Still, Mars is approaching the Earth and things will be a lot brighter by the end of the year.

My horoscopes are beginning to bore me but the money is good. Perhaps the time has come for a change in my life. The trouble with life is that youth comes too early in it. The trouble with dying is that you are so stiff the next day. These one-liners come to you by courtesy of my horoscope column what they appear at the bottom of.

Anyway, I need a break. I want to see old rustics playing dominoes and discussing Lloyd George in The Rat and Drainpipe. I want to see cricket on the village green and cows going to the lavatory. I want to remind myself what a hedge looks like.

Send me your answer quickly, Martin Lomax. We need someone who speaks the white man's tongue and rides like the wind. Either that or you could phone me.

Balzac said that men can resist sound argument but yield to a glance. Here's glancing at you.

Love,
Laurel

I phoned her.

I had not expected to hear her voice again and the giggle in it thrilled me.

'When are you coming down?' I asked.

'Sunday?' she suggested.

'What's wrong with Friday?'

'I have a dental appointment on Saturday. What is this life if full of caries! Listen, does abstinence make the heart grow fonder?'

'Certainly,' I said. 'Where have you been?'

She seemed strangely elusive on the phone; on the other hand, she seemed strangely elusive when she was in the room.

'I'm playing hard to get.'

'I thought you were playing impossible to get.'

She ignored this and asked, 'What will we do? Walk in the

country? Castrate a few bulls? Do moving pictures reach your part of the world?'

'Eventually.'

'The last one said "introducing Charlton Heston", I suppose?'

'Something like that.'

'Oh well, a saturnalian weekend then.'

'The Bali tries to please,' I assured her.

Lying on the bed now I wondered whether the intake of a few pills might help the coming debauchery, or maybe some fresh lettuces, which I had always believed to be an aid to male performance. The pleasant thoughts that this was leading me to were interrupted by the phone at the side of my bed. Lisa had switched through a call from my butcher, who reminded me in as friendly a way as he could manage that I had been overlooking some of his recent bills.

'The cheque's in the post,' I told him, and reflected, as I went downstairs to write it, that I had told the first of the three great lies. The second was, 'I won't come in your mouth.' I couldn't remember the third.

After I had written the cheque I decided that it was time for a tour of the premises, to see that everything was ready for another riotous Saturday evening. Scott was busy in the kitchen preparing some steaks, one of which I was going to need if the weekend's expectations were to be fulfilled. I went into the restaurant, where Judy was already laying the tables, and then back into the bar, where the shutters were down, protecting my valuable stock.

In the men's lavatories the graffiti artists on whom I waged a constant war had struck again. The new felt-nib pens must have been designed with just that market in mind.

I'M NINE INCHES LONG AND THREE INCHES THICK INTERESTED?

The inquiry in capital letters had elicited another question in small, prim handwriting underneath: Fascinated, but how big's your penis?

Hot water and a rag soon consigned this piquant dialogue to oblivion. The graffiti I was prepared to accept at the Bali was more up-market. Anybody who could drag in Krishnamurti or Baruch Spinoza had created a work that would endure — at least for a week.

I emerged satisfied that the hotel was ready once more to brighten people's lives, and what I saw from my side of the bar convinced me that they needed it. Watching them drowning their sorrows in here I am drawn again and again to the subversive conclusion that not many people are truly enjoying themselves. They reminisce nostalgically about the past and they talk hopefully about the future, but the present is always a necessary penance separating the two. Getting up tired, wasting the sunlit hours in an office or factory, going home worn out and slumping glassy-eyed in front of the television. Mounting bills, unrequited lusts, disillusioned wives, scornful kids. In the end even sex is too much trouble and it is lucky that most of them never find the time for enjoyment because they wouldn't know how to spend it if they did.

Not that I'm sympathetic. We arrive at our situation by a series of choices. It is the choices others make in the name of security that dismay me, but I can't tell them that as they give me their hard-earned wages to put in my Sharp electronic cash register.

5

Until that disastrous Saturday evening I had made only one serious mistake at the Bali Hotel.

A year earlier I had allowed myself to be persuaded that a discothèque should be installed at weekends. With my Majorcan experience fresh in my memory and being, anyway, more accustomed to the delicate felicity of the hand-jive than to the stomping, bopping chaos of the modern discothèque, I agreed reluctantly, and soon the bar was filled with raucous, unspeakable lyrics in quadraphonic supersound, and hard-faced young men who would scoop your eye out with an ashtray just to alleviate the boredom which seems to afflict the mentally under-privileged. I was too old for that sort of thing, and when a man utters those words he does so with relief and not regret.

The disco had to go and I invested in a Broadwood 1870 grand piano which I introduced to a young man called Mark, who not only wrote songs himself but could sing, on request, over four hundred of other people's. I was the owner of the only piano bar in the district and the piano bar was a hit. People who never came to the bar at any other time drove out on Saturday evenings to hear Mark singing the songs of Don McLean, Tim Hardin, Dan Hill and Simon and Garfunkel, and if they were people who occasionally had arguments, they kept them to themselves. The juke box was unplugged, the fruit machine silenced. There was plenty of floor space for dancing and it was much used. I nearly got into trouble though.

'Have you got a singing and dancing licence?' Adam asked me once.

'You need a licence to sing and dance in this country?' asked an American who was staying in the hotel.

'We'll need a sex permit soon,' Adam told him.

The following week I went to court and got a music licence. The Bali piano bar became famous, particularly in the summer, when people feel a mysterious need to cover miles after months of dark and rainy evenings spent indoors. They drove out to my hotel from some distances because this was the true countryside, where the horizon was high and green and many miles away and not a drab slate roof across the street. They walked along the river bank, conversing earnestly with swans and ducks, and then had cocktails on my patio. By the time they were lured into the bar by the siren songs of the resident musician they already looked much healthier than when they had arrived. They danced and they drank and occasionally they insisted on joining in and, if possible, taking over the singing themselves, although this was not something we encouraged: the average person's simple-hearted belief in the star-like quality of his own singing was, we discovered, one of the most prevalent delusions of our time.

Some dined first because it was a night out, but a serve-yourself, fixed-fee buffet that I introduced in the bar made much more than enough to pay for the music.

Early that evening I had more customers outside the bar than in it and I spent an hour providing a waiter service for the visitors who preferred to drink on the patio. In this capacity I received generous tips which I converted into alcohol later; all my drinks were meticulously paid for at the Bali.

When Lisa appeared I went into the kitchen for a salad. Scott was pouring potatoes into the peeling machine with extravagant abandon. Were potatoes cheap this week?

'Glad to see you,' he said. 'I'd like Monday off.'

'Bank holiday?' I said. 'I'll pay you extra.'

'You keep paying me extra so I never get a day off.'

He was quite right. I would much rather part with money than with him.

'I want to go to a motor-bike rally,' he said. 'I'll do the breakfasts before I go.'

'Do you think that when Escoffier worked at the Savoy he took afternoons off to go to motor-cycle rallies?'

Scott looked up to check that I was smiling. It was the age of the 'non-deferential work-force' and Scott, anyway, was a wild Marxist who would have unionized my staff in five minutes if I had any staff. Our relationship was as follows: I treated him like a king and he had me by the short hairs.

'Judy and I haven't had a day off for two weeks,' he said, fixing the lid of the potato machine.

'Nor have I,' I told him. 'One is never drained by work but only by idleness. Lack of work is the most enervating thing in the world. I'm quoting your favourite author, Mr Steinbeck.'

'Well, he never lived to enjoy his old age, did he?'

He switched on the machine, which made further conversation difficult, and I went across the kitchen to make myself a salad, mildly irritated at the prospect of having to do the cooking on Laurel's first day at the Bali. I didn't agree with Mr Steinbeck at all about work: it seemed an appalling waste of the short stay we have here. Not for the first time I wondered whether I should sell the hotel and invest the proceeds so that I could concentrate on the things that really mattered.

A breath-taking revelation by Mrs Stapleton was the early highlight of that evening. When I returned to the bar Adam was already half-way through his first pint. It always surprised me that he could find nothing better to do with his time: he travelled less than anyone I ever met. A trip to London was an adventure for him and foreign parts held unimaginable terrors. Adam was deeply suspicious of abroad and had never been there. You had the impression that if he was ever dragged screaming from this benighted island, his luggage would include guns, blow-pipes, snake bite serum and possibly the odd crucifix.

Mrs Stapleton sailed in, wearing the urchin-cut wig which she seemed to favour on Saturday evenings. She was wearing a yellow, orange and brown caftan, with an Indian silver pendant round her neck.

'Hallo, my old boiling-fowl,' said Adam. 'Let me fondle your artificial limb.'

She brushed him aside and sat majestically on a stool. 'A large Gordon's, Martin, please.'

'Somehow I don't think I fill Alice's head with romantic thoughts,' Adam said, emptying his glass.

'I imagine that you are to romance what lockjaw is to conversation,' said Mrs Stapleton. 'May I replenish your vessel?'

'A pint of lunatic's soup, please.'

'When do you eat? Or are you living solely on liquids?'

'Drink first, eat later,' said Adam. 'Tonight I shall be having a curry — I've put a toilet roll in the fridge.'

'I was thinking of our conversation of yesterday. It gave me doubts about your masculinity. I've decided that women don't appeal to you.'

'Oh, they do,' said Adam. 'Do you know which bit of them really turns me on? Pubic hair.'

'I'll bring you some down in the morning.'

Mark had arrived now and was warming up to the piano with a restrained version of 'American Pie'.

'If it is of any interest to you, gentlemen,' said Mrs Stapleton, 'today is my wedding anniversary.'

'Really?' I said, interested. She had never spoken about her marriage before. 'What did your husband do?'

'He was a soldier, a very fine soldier. He parachuted into Arnhem. All his friends were killed in the first two hours but he won a medal.'

'What happened to him?' Adam asked. 'I've often wondered.'

'He got eaten.'

Mrs Stapleton released this information without expression or emotion, while staring distantly into her large gin. For a moment I thought I had misheard her.

61

'He went to fight in the Congo twenty years ago. You remember the trouble there? I didn't want him to go but he had romantic notions about Africa although he had never seen the dirty place.'

'Who ate him?'

'His own platoon ate him.'

'His own platoon?' Adam said. 'But that's insubordination.'

'It might seem amusing to you, Adam. Forgive me if I don't laugh.'

This rebuke, delivered with icy politeness, created such embarrassment that I was relieved to be called away to serve a proletarian round of drinks to the man from the gas board. By the time I returned to Mrs Stapleton she was her normal self. I wanted to ask whether her husband having been eaten was the reason for her vegetarianism. It sounded like an interesting, far-from-everyday question, but I got no chance to ask it.

We had been joined by Rodney Pym and his second wife, Julie, both of whom made Adam visibly uneasy but for different reasons. He waged a continual and not very good-natured war on Rodney Pym, mainly, I suspected, because he fancied Mrs Pym.

'How is the vandalism coming along?' he asked when Rodney arrived at the bar.

Rodney smiled. 'It's awful what they are doing to our towns, isn't it, Adam?' he said. 'That's why I live in the country, as it happens. Much more pleasant. Do you know that I saw a crested crane on the way to work this morning?'

'How do you know it was on its way to work?' Mrs Stapleton asked gloomily.

Rodney Pym was a small, plump man with old-fashioned spectacles and an almost bald head. He was not yet thirty. The most significant fact about him — some said the only significant fact — was his wealth. He was one of those people who seem to be utterly devoid of talent but are, quite evidently, becoming richer before your eyes. The origins of his empire were obscure but one story was that he had inherited a street of houses from his father. Certainly his interests lay in property, particularly speculation and development. In many parts of the country old and lovely town centres were being reduced to rubble and replaced by supermarkets, multi-storey car parks and identical shop units. When this happened, many noughts were added to the estate of Rodney Pym. He had long since reached the stage where he had nothing to worry about beyond the annual re-stocking of his wine cellar and the acid-alkaline balance of his swimming-pool, but he still had a small office somewhere to which he drove every morning to run his continually expanding business.

A year earlier he had married Julie, a tall, silent and very beautiful girl whom Adam had been ineffectually lusting after. I had always regarded her as somewhat obtuse, an opinion I had to revise when I saw the speed at which she nailed Rodney's millions to the floorboards.

His first wife, a pale, dark-haired girl, had left him in hilarious circumstances. She failed to return from a holiday alone in southern Spain. Rodney flew out in a panic to find her and when he eventually ran her down, falling over drunkenly in a bar in Torremolinos, she had a deep tan and straw blonde hair and was attached, physically and emotionally, to a notoriously promiscuous fifteen-stone transvestite. That a woman could react to his nightly attentions in this way inflicted multiple wounds on Rodney's psyche and he was never quite the same pushy extrovert again. The following summer, with a face like a well-kept grave, he married Julie Tyrell in a registry office and guarded her thereafter like a dog.

Mrs Stapleton called Rodney 'a bore's bore' and said that he 'induced early glaze', but I saw him from a different viewpoint: the number of business lunches he had at the Bali made him one of my best customers.

'Hallo, Julie,' I said to his wife. She always looked at me rather nervously, as if I knew some terrible secret about her that I might blurt out at any moment. She gave me her usual wary smile now but didn't speak; she hardly ever did.

'Did you see my picture in the paper?' said Rodney. He belonged to the Rotarians and the Lions and several other organizations that managed to get his name or his picture in the newspaper every week. He seemed to feel that if your name didn't appear in a newspaper with some regularity you had ceased to exist; the idea that there were millions of people leading private, anonymous lives of total fulfilment was a heresy to him.

'I don't get the local paper,' Adam said.

'You must have one friend who could read it to you,' said Rodney, winking at me.

Surprisingly Adam didn't rise to this, and then I remembered that their best jousts had been fought when Julie wasn't there; her presence seemed to inhibit him.

'How are the poor, anyway?' Rodney went on. 'Still feeling that the world owes them something?'

'The world does owe me something,' Adam said. 'But it keeps giving it to someone else.'

'You could always kill yourself by jumping off Rodney's wallet,' suggested Mrs Stapleton. This idea evidently appealed to Rodney, who held up a fat wallet for inspection. He did not, however, offer to buy anyone a drink with its contents.

The Saturday night people had filled the bar now, prised from their televisions by the hope of fun. They were strangely quiet as Mark was singing a particularly beautiful song — 'Sometimes when we touch', I think it was.

I went up to Lisa, who was washing the glasses.

'Where are the Yorkshire contingent?' I asked.

'In the restaurant. They've been playing golf.'

'Are they all right?'

'That big bugger's an unpleasant sod.'

I was kept busy for some time by the exuberant thirsts of my customers, and when I returned to Mrs Stapleton's end of the bar I was surprised to discover that Adam and Julie were enmeshed on the dance floor.

'The cheeky bastard,' Rodney was saying. 'He didn't even ask my permission.' He turned to watch them: it was fairly smoochy stuff. 'You're running a sex orgy here, Martin.'

At one time the Bali did have a reputation of that sort. When the sexual quadrille reached feverish heights a year or more ago the hotel became known as The Clandestine Arrangement, but I discouraged the usage when I saw that it made women nervous.

'I've seen better orgies in a Methodist tent,' said Mrs Stapleton. 'Why don't you dance with me, Rodney, then you can intervene. It's heterosexual's excuse me.'

'I'm the wrong shape for dancing, as it happens,' said Rodney. 'Once I start I develop a momentum of my own.' He seemed unduly concerned about the couple on the floor.

'Do you think he fancies her?' he asked me.

'If I say No you'll be hurt, and if I say Yes you'll be angry,' I told him.

'I don't think he'd mind catching her as she got out of the bath,' observed Mrs Stapleton, who was never slow to fan the fire if she thought the evening was sagging. On her side of the counter I would probably have done the same.

'He could find his teeth embedded in his tonsils,' Rodney muttered. I smothered a laugh: Rodney was not a man who radiated menace.

'Anyone would think they were copulating on the piano,' I said.

'He wants her. I'm sure of it. Funny — I hadn't noticed before.'

This wasn't the protective love of a newly wed speaking: it was the voice of a man accustomed to hanging on to his possessions.

'I've changed my mind, Alice. Let's dance.'

'Not too energetically, I hope,' Mrs Stapleton said, getting off her stool. 'At my age you can break a rib with a cough.'

They drifted off to a half-remembered song and when I next looked Adam was dancing with Mrs Stapleton, her wig only slightly askew, and a murderously solemn Rodney had reclaimed his bride of twelve months.

Adam was first back.

'I need a drink that will knock your socks off,' he said.

'That man should be hanged with piano wire.'

'He's not that pleasant, I must admit,' said Mrs Stapleton. 'It's hard to believe that he was once, or so he says, a blue-eyed, blond-headed baby.'

'Now he's a red-eyed, bald-headed idiot,' said Adam. 'I've just heard some very unpleasant facts about his private life.'

'I can hear you,' I said, moving closer. 'We've been a bit short of gossip lately.' But we were deprived of a few scurrilous details from Adam by the coarse tones of Edwin Catchpole, who was now announcing, 'You can pour this beer back in the horse.'

'I wonder which charm school he went to?' said Mrs Stapleton.

'What's your problem?' I said to the Catchpole party.

'The beer tastes like horse piss,' said Catchpole.

'How extraordinary,' said Mrs Stapleton. 'They drink horse piss in Yorkshire.'

I took Catchpole's pint and held it up to the light. It looked like syrup.

'I'll change the barrel,' I said. 'I won't be a minute.'

I went down the steps behind the bar to the cellar. There were plenty of barrels ready on the racks and I transferred the pipes. The beer was driven upstairs by three different methods. Gas cylinders forced some of the lager up, and an electric motor drove some of the beer. A third beer was sucked upstairs to the thirsty customers by the pump itself.

Catchpole's pint when it eventually arrived was, I regret to say, flawless.

The cheerful messages from the Broadwood 1870 were not, it soon emerged, to the Yorkshire party's taste, and they withdrew noisily to a neglected corner of the room where a pack of cards was produced by one of their number, and pound notes soon covered the table. The law on playing cards for money in a public bar is as ambiguous as it is stupid and I ignored the newly formed card school and listened to the music. I am running an hotel and not a boarding school.

Once, when one of the players came over for a round of

66

drinks, I helped carry pint mugs to their table and saw that most of the money was stacked neatly in front of Catchpole while his friends sat glumly hoping for better cards. For a while I stood and watched their game. It was stud poker and Catchpole's calling was remorselessly accurate.

'You're bluffing,' he growled when one man, who could have had a straight, put £50 on the table. 'I'll raise you £50.' The player capitulated.

At one o'clock Mark abandoned the piano, accepted £25 in tax-free notes and disappeared into the night. At two o'clock only Catchpole's party were left in the bar, still capable, apparently, of drinking whatever was set before them — horse liniment, hair lacquer, liquid boot polish. As they were residents it was difficult to close the shop. They were legally entitled to whatever drinks they wanted, and a more extravagant hotel owner would have had a night porter ferrying bottles to their rooms. I economized on the night porter and forfeited my sleep.

Catchpole had won £130 at cards and was now buying the drinks for his victims.

'You're the champ,' said one of them. 'You ought to play in the clubs.'

'Week after week he takes my money,' said the soap opera star. 'Still, I've got to win one day.'

'No, you haven't,' said Catchpole.

At three o'clock only Catchpole and the soap opera star, who turned out to be Gordon Hammerdale, remained. The rest of their party had disappeared, one by one, so fearful of abuse at not lasting the distance that they didn't even say good-night. It had reached the stage now where I could only wonder at the two survivors' capacities. There had been some drinkers at the Bali, but these two were moving into areas where records are broken.

'Great to get away,' Gordon Hammerdale said, 'from the bloody kids.'

'Gordon's got six kids,' Catchpole said in my direction. His eyes didn't seem to be focusing properly and I can only imagine the blurred picture he was receiving.

'Not going to be any more though. Found out what's causing it.'

'He's changed his bloody milkman,' Catchpole said, and laughed so much he nearly fell off his stool.

'Didn't even want to get married,' Gordon Hammerdale said. 'She just moved in on me.'

'You bloody asked her,' Catchpole said accusingly.

'Mavis?' said Gordon Hammerdale. 'I bloody never asked her. She insinuated herself.'

'She what?' Catchpole said, steadying himself by holding the bar.

'Suddenly there were plants everywhere. The bloody house started to go green. There was a red toothbrush in the bathroom and I knew mine was blue. I went to the airing cupboard for socks and found a bra. I thought: Mavis is living with me.'

'It ruined his golf,' Catchpole said. 'Gordon was a scratch golfer at fifteen.'

'You play?' Gordon Hammerdale asked me.

I shook my head.

'No time,' I told him.

'Long hours, is it?'

I answered by looking at my watch, but he didn't understand.

'Give me a tequali sunrise,' he said. 'It'll set me up for tomorrow.'

'I'll have a kummel,' said Catchpole. 'I've had everything else.' He lowered himself carefully from the stool and went over to the cigarette machine on the wall. Its mechanism defeated him and I had to get the cigarettes for him. He fumbled with the packet impatiently, eventually producing a cigarette which he put in his mouth the wrong way, lighting the filter tip. He swore, crushed it in an ashtray, and started again.

'Have one yourself,' Gordon Hammerdale said when I produced his tequila sunrise. I fetched myself a Bells and decided that I deserved it. My drinking began slowly every evening because I never knew how long the evening would last, but I reckoned that it was safe now to have a couple of Scotches. I thought that if, as a result of this late drinking, Catchpole woke tomorrow with a splitting head it would all have been worthwhile. He seemed to be fighting now to keep his eyes open, the way that people who have drunk too much Scotch often do. His attempts to reach the ashtray with his cigarette ash were missing every time.

'When are you playing golf tomorrow?' I asked. 'Or today, as it now is.'

'Ten o'clock,' Catchpole said. 'What time is it?'

'Half-past three.'

'Let's make it eleven o'clock,' Gordon Hammerdale said. 'May not feel too good in the morning.'

'It's fixed,' Catchpole said. 'Ten o'clock.'

Gordon Hammerdale looked at his half-drunk tequila and stood up.

'Bed then,' he said. 'Thought it was earlier.'

He walked unsteadily to the door without saying goodbye.

'Can't take it,' Catchpole said with a sneer. 'He's got six kids, you know.'

'Yes.'

'He was a scratch golfer at fifteen.'

'You told me.'

'I'll have a whisky.'

I gave him a Bells. He didn't offer me one. I sat on my side of the bar studying him. Now we were alone, but he was too drunk to recognize his own brother.

'You the owner?' he asked, not looking at me.

I told him I was.

'Money in it?'

I looked for the answer that he would like least.

'A hell of a lot,' I said.

He thought about it and then, evidently, considered his own financial situation. 'This little weekend is going to clean me out,' he said. 'I'm a drunken bum.' He had reached the maudlin stage.

I had another whisky and decided that it would be the last.

I was beginning to feel fairly light-headed myself. If Catchpole wanted another drink I would offer him a prussic acid cocktail. The evening had gone on too long and through the window I could see a hint of dawn.

'Know what I do Saturdays?' Catchpole said suddenly.

'What's that?' I asked.

'Chuck up on the compost heap. Every Saturday. Regular as clockwork.'

I managed to convey, I think, how fascinating this information was to me, deciding at the same time to get the bar closed quickly.

'Every Saturday. Never miss.' He smiled proudly at his reliability.

I finished my whisky and stood up.

'Regular as clockwork,' he said. 'Course, I drink more at home.'

I put my glass in the sink and looked at his. It was empty.

'One more whisky,' he said. He hadn't said please all night.

'The bar is closed,' I said.

He looked confused.

'What?'

'Closed. *Cerrado. Fermé. Geschlossen.*'

'Geschlossen? I was in Germany.'

'You were?' I said.

'Yeah. Those were the days.' Then he remembered what he wanted. 'One more whisky.' He held the glass in my face. I took it from him, put it down and told him again that the bar was closed.

He banged the counter with his fist and stood up.

'Give me a whisky,' he repeated. 'You bloody southerner.'

I remembered the abortive search of Yorkshire police for a hit and run driver, but just as his anger seemed likely to explode the skin on his face became taut and the colour faded from his cheeks. And then, without a sound, he keeled over backwards, his body remaining almost straight, and banged the back of his head on the floor. I was beside him at once to check his breathing but it was quite normal. He lay on his

70

back like a boxer who had lost concentration for a moment and walked into an uppercut.

I locked the till and pulled down the grille which protected the bar's stocks, and then I went round the room switching off the lights. By eight o'clock my cleaning lady would have restored the place to pristine freshness.

With a hand under each armpit I began to drag Edwin Catchpole across the floor. He was even heavier than he looked, and after two huge efforts his recumbent form had moved no further than twelve feet and I was exhausted.

For a while I sat on a bar stool getting my breath back and wondering whether to wake one of his friends. There were thirty-eight steps between the bar and room seven and I realized that it would take more than one man to carry him there. I sat there for some time hoping that he would come round and be able to make the journey on his own, but presently it became apparent that this was not likely.

Then I had the idea and was so delighted that I sat alone laughing out loud at my own brilliance. Of course, the whisky, which affects the lower part of the brain which has ideas, was my ally and inspiration.

Two minutes later I was in the cellar, clearing out the wine stocks and the spirits and champagne that were stacked in my father's cell. Old English wines that nobody was ever going to ask for — Birch, Beeswin, Muscadine and Sloe — and dozens of bottles of Cloberg and Mouton Cadet were hastily shifted to other parts of the cellar. Cartons of vodka that had been enthusiastically over-ordered after a misleading article in the trade press followed, and then I carried three bottles of Chivas Regal out after them.

When the cell was empty I returned to my unconscious guest, who lay, mouth open, where I had left him.

Enthusiasm gave me new energy now and I dragged him with surprising ease behind the counter and down the stone steps. He was wearing a cheap blue suit, rather formal I thought for a holiday weekend, and I can't promise that the fabric didn't suffer during the journey across the cellar floor.

71

But I was in a hurry and scared that the movement would wake him. I needn't have worried.

In the cell I laid him gently on the ground, removed myself quickly and locked the door. I put the key in my pocket and stood there for a few minutes, amid the barrels and the boxes and the plastic tubes, enjoying the sight of Corporal Catchpole behind bars.

On my side of them, I noticed, was the pack of cards that he had been using. They had fallen from his pocket during his travels across the floor. Returning them to him now seemed an unnecessary risk and I put them in my own pocket and headed for the steps.

I would like to have been there to see his expression when he discovered his situation, but it was four o'clock now and I didn't think that I would be able to make it.

Part Three

Sunday

6

On Sunday mornings I placed six bottles of champagne in ice buckets at one end of the counter and next to them I stood a huge jug of fresh orange juice to tempt my customers with Buck's Fizz. On Sunday mornings the strange array of drinks that were lined up on the shelf behind me — the Jim Beam bourbon, the Old Bushmills Irish whiskey, the Sake — were ignored.

The first customer, regardless of the depredations of the night before, was always Adam, and he came in this morning wearing jeans and a tartan shirt, a long slim cigar tucked into one side of his mouth like Clint Eastwood about to ride off into the sun with a wagon-load of corpses. As he climbed on a stool, Mrs Stapleton came in behind him and took the next seat.

'You're all late,' I said. 'You wouldn't be late for church, would you?'

'This isn't a church, thank goodness,' said Mrs Stapleton. 'Campari, please, Martin.'

'It is on Sunday,' I said, 'and you are my congregation.'

'I haven't prayed since my dog died,' said Mrs Stapleton. 'I was fourteen. There is no life after death. That's definite.'

'Is there life after breakfast?' said Adam, holding his head.

'You raise an interesting metaphysical question there,' said Mrs Stapleton, handing me money. 'I'm not at my best myself during the *ante meridiem* hours.'

I poured myself a Buck's Fizz and then gave it to Adam. He looked like a man in need of an injection.

'I think I'll go into hospital and have my wheels changed round,' he said.

Mrs Stapleton studied him. 'What time did you get to bed?' she asked.

'Four o'clock.'

'Blimey, I was getting up for my second pee then.' She put her mouth to the straw, which went red and then white and then red again as she sucked her campari. 'You shouldn't drink so much if it makes you depressed.'

'Depression is quite natural,' said Adam between sips. 'We cry at birth but it takes months to learn to laugh.'

'There's always someone worse off than yourself, and it's always Adam,' I said.

I poured myself a Buck's Fizz and gazed out of the window in search of customers, but it was only the dedicated few who were out this early on a Sunday morning. I went over to the juke box in the corner and put it on free play so that customers would not be deterred from providing music by the huge expense. The titles all referred to the same thing: 'Am I Ever Going To Hold You Again?' 'You Know That I Love You!' 'Don't Let Go!' 'Love You Inside Out!' What a brain-washed mob song-writers are — why didn't they stretch their talents to lyrics about building a motorway, winning a squash match or losing your driving licence? I put on Abba.

Two residents, an old couple who had opted for a bank holiday in the country, arrived to ask for coffee. At full volume the Gaggia coffee machine rivalled a juggernaut's air brakes and for a while we lost Abba.

'I've made a decision, Adam, dear,' said Mrs Stapleton when the lonely coffee-drinkers had shuffled off to the other end of the bar. 'I'm going to regard it as my mission to find you the perfect woman. There are plenty of them about.'

Adam smiled. 'There are also four-leaf clovers. As far as I'm concerned the perfect woman is the one who is there after eight pints. In fact, I phoned one after eight pints last night and asked her whether a fuck was absolutely out of the question. Unfortunately, she confirmed that it was.'

'I don't like that word much,' said Mrs Stapleton. 'I don't

mind it, but I don't like it much.'

'Think of it as one of the first acronyms,' I said. 'They used to write For Unlawful Carnal Knowledge on the charge lists at court.'

'Acronyms?' said Mrs Stapleton. 'Don't mention acronyms to me.'

She shivered at some awful memory.

'What have you got against them?' I asked.

'Haven't you heard my tragic story? A few years ago when I became fed up with reading about kittens being drowned I organized an animal rescue team to look after the creatures until a home could be found. To emphasize to the mean sods who live round here that it wouldn't cost them anything, I called it the Free Animal Rescue Team. I went to see our local paper to get the necessary publicity and that Friday they had a headline that said "Give Alice's FART a Big Welcome". The sub-editor got the sack, the paper banned any further mention of us and the venture folded amid a cackle of laughter. So much for my experience of acronyms.'

'You don't want to hear the sad story of an old friend of mine who went to work for the Trade Unions' Research Department?' I asked.

'No, I don't,' she said. 'Get me a drink.'

I poured her a Campari and myself a Buck's Fizz and asked Adam whom he had phoned.

'Julie,' he said, as if I should have guessed.

'Julie? Did Rodney know?'

He shrugged. 'Don't mention that man to me, pal. He beats her up. He beats his wives like dinner gongs. That's what turned the last one against men.'

'How do you know that?' I asked.

'I talked to Julie in here last night. And when he wants to make it up, do you know what he does?'

'Tell me,' I said. Nobody had told me anything today so far.

'He buys her expensive bottles of perfume and leaves one on each step of the staircase. On the top step he leaves a cheque for a hundred pounds.'

'Well, I never,' said Mrs Stapleton.

'That is the great institution of marriage that you are urging on your friends. It's enough to make your hair curl.'

'I don't want curly hair,' said Mrs Stapleton. 'But I believe that I know more about marriage than you do, young man.'

'I know about it,' said Adam. 'Duck a swing, block a hook, catch a kick. Rodney's first wife once threw eleven bottles of Babycham at him in a small room and missed with every one.'

Mrs Stapleton considered this episode for some time. 'The mistake we make is basing it on romantic love,' she said. 'Historically, that's a very recent idea. More practical considerations used to apply and marriages lasted longer. I watched two people making love once, in a film in Hong Kong. It really is the most absurd activity. All that stroking, groaning, writhing and panting. I'd sooner play draughts. Let me buy drinks.'

I filled their glasses, and the newly exposed wife-beater walked in.

'Good morning, Rodney,' I said.

Killers, rapists, traitors, wife-beaters — all were welcome here if they brought pieces of paper bearing the Queen's picture.

'What a night!' he said. 'What a night! I got breath-tested on the way home.'

'What was the verdict?'

'Halitosis, I should imagine,' said Mrs Stapleton, over her Campari.

'Negative, luckily. Buck's Fizz, please. I don't think the copper had ever seen a Monteverdi before.'

'What's a Monteverdi?' asked Mrs Stapleton.

'My Swiss car,' said Rodney. 'I remember getting home and telling my wife that she was the rock on which my life rested.'

'Or foundered,' said Mrs Stapleton.

'Where is this rock?' asked Adam. 'Slaving over a hot stove?'

'Not at all. We are lunching at the Cloche Hat. If anyone would like to come as my guest they'd be welcome. Martin?'

'I don't know,' I said. I was surprised by the invitation.

Rodney didn't buy lunch for anybody unless there was business in it.

'What would I have to offer to persuade you?'

'Girls jumping out of cakes?' I suggested.

'Adam?'

Adam looked wary, but Julie would be there. 'Okay,' he said.

'If you're paying, include me in,' said Mrs Stapleton.

I managed to accept Rodney's invitation in a manner which left no doubt that the generosity was all mine. The truth was that bank holiday weekends were notoriously quiet at the Bali Hotel. For many of my hard-working clientele they provided a rare break and the list of absentees was depressingly long.

The Starkeys, Nick and Penny, who had been trying for six years to have a baby, were trying this weekend in Puerto Banus; Denzil Kirby and Sharon, whom everyone imagined wrongly to be married, were, with characteristic economy, camping in the New Forest; Bill Taylor, who had made half a million pounds out of fruit machines, was languishing, for the second time this year, on the coral-fringed beaches of Sri Lanka. (It was Bill who had been thrown off the committee of his residents' association after urging that the funds should be sunk in vintage champagne and the annual meeting held in Monte Carlo.)

Tim Westbrook, who had a vasectomy and then lost both his children in a car accident, had taken his grieving wife to an air show in Devon; another air-lover, Paul Hawkins, a British Airways pilot, was in Los Angeles for a few hours; two-ton Tony Melville, who could drink three pints of beer in twenty-seven seconds, was doing the thing he did best at a beer festival just outside Brussels; the Urquharts were weekending at the Hotel Cervantes in Paris; the Maxwell-Drapers, who kept a boat on the river, had sailed off in it; Frankie Witney, whose wife died on a squash court, had left — sports mania unabated — for a cricket tour in the Midlands; Alison, who was jokily known at the Bali as *la tarte maison*, was in the burns unit of the local hospital after falling asleep under her sun lamp; and Barry and Janice Nind, who had more sense than to travel during a holiday weekend, were themselves lumbered by two ageing houseguests, the parents of one of them, who were militant Presbyterians and manic about hooch.

Some Sunday lunchtime drinkers did eventually drift in along with a few of that strange breed who jump in their cars and head for the sea on the days when the roads are most crowded. I was waiting for Moaner Lisa to finish her chambermaiding and relieve me of bar duties so that I could mingle with my customers and make them feel appreciated, even interesting. I was adept at this and also at encouraging faster drinking; nobody was going to be carried from my bar suffering from dehydration.

I once formulated the Laws of Bars and considered having them printed for national distribution. I can only remember the first two now — my memory is not my strongest suit. Law one was: The most boring person will talk the most. The second law was: The last round of drinks is always the most expensive. I regarded it as my duty to keep these laws in mind and minimize their damage. A recital of law two had many a meanie reaching into his pocket quite early in the evening, and recalling law one always restored the conversational balance.

When there was a lull in the orders I moved back to my drink at the end of the bar. A barman could eavesdrop any conversation and frequently overhear the most astonishing confidentialities without people minding. It wasn't very flattering.

'Rodney thinks that poverty is some kind of personality defect,' Adam was complaining.

Rodney, in black silk roll-neck shirt and a pale blue denim suit that looked more expensive than denim suits normally looked, said, 'This is like having mountaineering lessons from a man with vertigo. What you know about finance could be written in headline type on a flea's nuts.'

'I'm on the side of the poor, the depressed and the ethnically outnumbered,' said Adam.

'You're not ethnically outnumbered, are you?' asked Mrs

80

Stapleton. 'You look vaguely Caucasian to me.'

'No, but I'm poor and depressed.'

'You'll be lecturing me on how to handle women next,' Rodney said. A certain edge had entered his voice.

'I don't think so,' said Mrs Stapleton. 'Adam regards women as mice regard kestrels.'

'Is that so?' said Rodney. 'I hear he is a bit of an expert.'

He obviously wanted to start something, but Adam wasn't going to let him.

'Not me,' he said. 'I was put off marriage at an early age — my parents were married. Anyway, I don't think the interests of men and women coincide much, so it only means one side has to keep making sacrifices.'

'What are these interests,' demanded Mrs Stapleton, 'which exclude women?'

'Evenings devoted to drinking your way along one shelf, poker games that stop for breakfast. That sort of thing.'

'The truth is that you don't want women to share your interests, Adam,' said Mrs Stapleton.

Adam agreed willingly. 'Of course I don't. It wouldn't be natural. I like riding horses on the common but I don't take them home to watch television. And that's why I've never tried marriage.'

'I read somewhere that a man should be prepared to try everything once, with the possible exceptions of sodomy and folk dancing,' said Mrs Stapleton to me.

I nodded agreement at this baffling proposition and turned to watch Rodney. He seemed to have found Adam's apparent indifference to women deeply reassuring.

'The way you think, it's lucky for the opposite sex that you haven't tried it,' he said.

'Satan rebukes Beelzebub,' murmured Mrs Stapleton. 'What do you think, Martin?'

'Nothing ages a man quicker than a trip up the aisle,' I said. I said it lightly: Laurel was already on her way to the Bali Hotel.

A demand for drinks called me away and when I returned they were squabbling over who should buy the next round.

Mrs Stapleton refused, having bought the last one, Adam said he had no money, and Rodney protested that he was paying for the lunch. It became necessary for me to buy them.

'To my mother's only son, God bless him,' said Rodney, holding up his Buck's Fizz. 'What time are we all going to the Cloche Hat?'

Lisa came in.

'Sorry I'm late,' she said. I stepped back to let her behind the bar and she went past, her smell following her like a dog.

'By the way,' she said, 'nobody slept in room seven.'

'Room seven?'

'It's supposed to be a Mr Catchpole.'

I hadn't given him a thought all morning. One day I will forget to put my shoes on.

My guest in the oubliette had taken one shoe off. He was lying on the floor on his back with the shoe as his suede pillow.

As I came down the steps towards him, rehearsing my apologies and explanations and prepared, if necessary, to forget his weekend bill, he raised himself on his elbow and stared at me, blank-faced, through the bars that separated us.

I was advancing, key in hand, when he jumped to his feet, a surprisingly athletic movement in one so large, and moved towards me, oozing hostility from every pore.

The rehearsed explanation ('I was drunk. You were drunk. We understand') suddenly seemed less than adequate — it was quite apparent that just after I unlocked the door he would break my neck.

I returned the key to my pocket and examined his dishevelled appearance. His smart suit was in urgent need of a clean after his night on the dirty floor.

His eyes followed the vanishing key. 'It's some sort of joke, is it?' he said. 'Well, just unlock the door and I'll show you a joke. After that, we'll call the police.'

I walked away from him to a beer crate in the corner of our dark dungeon and sat down, to think.

'That puts a new light on things,' I said. The new light showed me that whatever I did now I was going to lose. My only chance was to win him over, to persuade him of the hilarity of it all, but his manner did not suggest that this programme was destined for success.

I said, 'If you are going to call the police, I may as well let you out tomorrow as today.'

I wondered what evidence he would have if he went to the police and I denied his story. He had urinated against the wall, I noticed — perhaps the forensic department could ruin me with that.

'Why would you want to do that?' he asked. He had shed some aggression, realizing, presumably, that other tactics were needed.

'Because I haven't got time to deal with the police today,' I said. 'I'm going out to lunch in a minute and my girl-friend is arriving this afternoon.'

'Unlock the door first,' he said evenly.

I considered it — I wanted to get the incident over — but I couldn't forget the story of the police looking for a hit-and-run driver after Catchpole had beaten somebody up. Unlocking the door now would be like jumping in front of a train.

A new idea arrived to quell my mounting panic. If I left him without food today he would hardly emerge like a raging lion: I might even have to help him up the steps. Then I would push a few hundred pounds into his hand and send him back to wherever he festered in Yorkshire.

'Unlock the door and get my head beaten in?' I said. 'I'm afraid you're not taking this joke in the right spirit, Mr Catchpole. You've got no sense of humour and it's posing certain problems.'

I felt more confident now that I had decided what to do.

'Look,' he said, in the friendliest tone he had used, 'let's talk about it.'

I could see that he now thought that he had a madman on his hands; it was a reasonable conclusion in the situation.

'Okay,' I said.

'Just unlock the door and I'll go upstairs and we'll say no more about it. I'm supposed to be playing golf this morning.'

'It's afternoon. You've missed it.'

I saw him again as a burly sadist, systematically beating up men whose misdemeanours scarcely deserved a verbal rebuke.

'Anyway,' he said, resigned to the lost golf, 'what do you say?' He clutched the bars with his huge hands. They looked as hard as ever.

'What I say is that if I let you out of that door now I'll be in hospital by this evening,' I said. 'I put you in there as a joke, and I came down to let you out. But . . .'

'I can't see any bloody joke,' he snarled, and then controlled himself. 'Is there any chance of a drink or something while we discuss this? I've got a mouth like an old boot.'

'You'll only foul the cell,' I told him.

'Cell?' The word distracted him. 'This is the cellar, not a cell.'

'Well, it's a cell now and you're in it.'

He looked at me strangely and I could only guess at what memories were being stirred.

'Do you want money?' he asked suddenly. 'Is that what you want?'

'I have plenty, thanks.' I imagined that any money that passed between us as a result of this farce would be travelling the other way.

'I wish I had.'

'What's your job, Mr Catchpole?'

'I'm a salesman, a rep. Pies, sausages, bacon.' He was trying to be civil now to keep me talking. He had no other choice.

'Yes, I can see you selling sausages,' I said.

His fat, pink, piggy face would find its natural setting above a tray of fat, pink pork sausages.

'Are you married?' I asked.

He shook his head. 'Not any more.'

'You hit her too much?' I suggested.

His expression said it was a bull's-eye.

'She was a stupid bitch,' was all he would say. 'Look, how long is this joke going on? I've come all this way to play golf.'

'Your mates don't seem to have missed you,' I said.

He shook his head wonderingly. Then he found a new approach.

'Look, leave me the key and go. I can't hit you if you're not here, can I?'

'What are you suggesting — that I leave my own hotel?'

He held his hand up, and I remembered thinking in Germany 'a man's hand no bigger than a cloud'.

'I promise,' he said. 'I don't hit people.'

'Well,' I said, 'you've hit me.' He stared at me curiously, and I added: 'Corporal.'

He was so surprised that he took several paces backwards and then sat on the dirty floor.

'Ah,' he said. 'I've got it.'

'Good,' I said.

'I thought there was something familiar about your face. Lomax, isn't it? LAC Lomax?'

I nodded.

'Bugger me,' he said, and started shaking his head again. 'I've always remembered you because you were the only prisoner who said we'd meet again.'

'Hallo again,' I said.

The revelation had literally floored him, but I had to admire the intelligence of his reaction.

'Okay, I get the joke now.' He smiled for the first time. 'I see what you're up to. Fair enough. We're quits.'

That may have been my only chance to emerge unscathed from the ludicrous predicament that I had created. If it was, I muffed it. Perhaps he really would have walked peacefully upstairs and regarded all debts between us as having been paid. But I wasn't convinced.

'Not yet, we're not,' I said.

'I was court-martialled,' he told me, evidently forgetting that I was the principal witness.

'And found not guilty,' I replied. 'Boy, you lied like a politician. It was impressive to watch.'

'Not my fault if they believed me rather than you.'

85

'They always believe a policeman,' I said, 'even in civil courts.'

He thought about that for a time and then stood up and came back to the bars.

'So what are we going to do, Mr Lomax? Don't you think the joke is over?'

I could see him now in his cheese-cutter hat with the white top that meant RAF policeman and surprising reserves of hatred, not all of it for him, swept back. When I was twenty I was seething with anger with the British government for wasting two years of my life in the Royal Air Force, but by the time I was thirty I had wasted ten more on my own without their help. There seemed to be a perfect justice in leaving him there for a bit longer, a very brief taste of the medicine that he had dispensed more violently. He had been there for nine hours now, and I told myself that whatever consequences I was going to face for this madness would be no worse tomorrow than today. The joke was growing on me as the memories returned.

'No, I don't,' I said.

His face twitched a little as he wrestled with the possibility of threats, but he seemed to get a grip on himself and gave me a resigned look.

'Any chance of some food while we discuss this?' he asked. 'I'm paying enough for this weekend.'

'We'll revise your bill later,' I said. 'The pleasure is all mine.'

'What about some food, then?'

'Eat dirt,' I said. 'Give a boost to the anti-bodies.'

I was beginning to derive a sick enjoyment from his plight. But at the same time I had a growing feeling that roses were not what I was going to come out of this smelling of.

'You have a reputation for violence, Edwin,' I said. 'It makes a chap nervous.'

'You're a raving bloody lunatic,' he said, losing control. He walked round the cell, banging the walls with his fists as if the bricks would crumble before his strength.

'You have a violent mouth, too,' I said. 'But luckily I don't have to listen to it.'

I stood up. The beer crate was far from comfortable.

'Don't go,' he said quickly. 'What can I offer? What do you want?'

'Revenge,' I said simply. 'I'm quite happy to leave the situation as it is.'

'Revenge?' said Catchpole. 'Twenty years ago! I had forgotten all about it.'

'I nearly had too,' I admitted. 'Let us remind ourselves.'

I took the newspaper cuttings that I had found in the photograph album from my wallet and read one out to him:

> Corporal Edwin Catchpole, a twenty-one-year-old RAF policeman, pleaded not guilty yesterday to twenty-four charges of ill-treating prisoners in the detention barracks of Wahn air base, near Cologne, Germany.
>
> A court-martial was told that split lips and black eyes were the order of the day at the Field Punishment Detention Unit where airmen were drilled until they dropped, fed syrup in mess tins until they were sick and forced to shave while running on the spot, cutting their faces.
>
> Wing-Commander Richard Bate said Catchpole was guilty of 'brutal and cowardly acts' that had gone on for months.
>
> The case continues today.

'And I was acquitted,' said Catchpole.

'Well, don't tell me,' I said. 'I still remember the black eye. How about this?'

I found another cutting:

> An airman demonstrated a Russian torture to a court-martial yesterday by standing four feet from a wall and then

leaning against it with the middle fingers of each hand bearing his weight.

The court refused an invitation from the prosecution to try it 'to see what pain it causes'.

Edwin Catchpole, an RAF police corporal, has pleaded not guilty at Wahn, Rhineland, to twenty-four charges of ill-treating airmen, including the Russian torture.

Mr Terry Devaney, defending, asked the court to consider whether this punishment was any worse than doubling for an hour, which was permitted by detention camp regulations.

'The prosecution would have us believe that what was going on in this prison rivalled Belsen,' said Mr Devaney.

And another:

An RAF corporal forced a British soldier to lick his boots, a court-martial was told at Wahn, near Bonn, yesterday.

The same corporal poured soup over another man, drilled men until they collapsed exhausted and beat them regularly, it was alleged.

Mr Terry Devaney, defending, said that Corporal Edwin Catchpole, who faces twenty-four charges of ill-treatment, was being made the scapegoat for a disgraceful state of affairs at the camp.

I pushed the cuttings through the bars, but he didn't pick them up.

'You need something to read,' I said. 'It passes the time.'

'I could murder a bacon sandwich,' said the much-maligned

custodian of the law. 'Look, you can't be worrying about that stuff after all these years can you?'

'I hadn't given it a thought until you arrived.'

'I had to pick this hotel.'

I nodded sympathetically. 'It was rather an unlucky strike for a man who usually strikes so accurately.'

I looked at my watch. It was time for me to make a tactful tour of the kitchen to see how Scott was progressing. Despite his monarchical powers, he graciously allowed me to wander about his kingdom and even make the occasional observation. However, with most of our guests on the golf course and another on involuntary hunger strike it would be a very quiet lunch hour.

'What happened last night, anyway?' Catchpole asked.

'You were drunk,' I said.

'The last thing I remember was thinking "This must stop". Do you drink?'

'Yes, but I'm not in your class. You passed out.'

He shook his head. 'Not for the first time. How did you get me here, wherever we are?'

'I dragged you. You're greatly overweight — it's a problem which we at the Bali Hotel are proposing to help you with.'

'If I miss meals I get headaches,' he said, rather pathetically.

'Headaches I owe you,' I told him. 'Why don't you read your press cuttings? You used to be famous.'

He picked them up and put them in his pocket without looking at them.

'No one at home knows about that,' he said. 'They're not great newspaper readers up there.' He thought of something. 'None of my mates knows.'

'I won't tell them,' I promised. 'We try not to bore our guests.'

He looked relieved.

'It stopped me getting in the police,' he said. 'The police was always my ambition.'

'But you were found not guilty!'

'They study your records, and a court-martial leaves a stain whatever the result. They rejected me. They don't have to say why.'

'And now you sell sausages.'

'We can't all be rich.'

The political note gave me pause, I admit, but the sight of those big hands clutching the bars, the white knuckles more than four inches wide, reminded me quickly where safety lay.

His fluctuating mood seemed to have settled now for a chatty resignation.

'A lot of money in hotels, is there?'

'Enough,' I said, 'if you watch your overheads.'

'We picked you out of the AA book. Your rates are very reasonable.'

I nodded. 'I don't imagine that you will be writing to them to endorse their recommendation.'

He seemed to take this seriously. 'I'll write the letter now if you unlock the door.' He looked at me as if he thought that he had suddenly solved our problem.

'We're not that desperate for clients,' I told him. 'I could live off the takings at the bar.'

Looking at him then, and wondering how I was going to get him out of the cellar without myself sustaining horrendous injuries or creating embarrassing scenes upstairs when he appeared, I had a couple of ideas.

The first was that I should release him in the middle of the night while the world slept, and the second was that he would be less likely to tear my limbs off if he was unconscious.

A third possibility, of having some of my larger friends with me when I unlocked the door, I discarded quickly: if he did go to the police I would have provided him with witnesses of the débâcle.

I cheered up considerably. I would provide him with drink until he was unconscious. If necessary I would slip something into his drink to make quite sure that he was. Then, in the middle of the night, I would drag him, with

Scott's help, up to room seven, where he would wake with a mega-hangover tomorrow. I might even be able to convince him that he had dreamt the whole thing. The problem was solved.

'I'll come and see you later,' I said, feeling much more hopeful about how it was going to end.

'Where are you going?'

'I have to see how the luncheon preparations are coming along.'

'And you're leaving me here?' He asked the question as if he had never expected it to happen.

'I don't have much choice, do I? Why don't you stand four feet from the wall and lean against it for half an hour on two fingers. Go on — enjoy yourself. This time next week you could be in your grave.'

It was a remark that I often made, but in the dank darkness of the cellar it didn't carry the usual light-hearted ring.

7

I was the unproud owner of a slightly bruised Peugeot 504 estate car, metallic green plus grime, hardly the traditional limousine of a prosperous hotelier on the make but highly suitable for the quantity of shopping that I did myself every weekday morning at the market, the cash-and-carry, the wine merchants or the butchers.

Mrs Stapleton elected wisely to travel to the Cloche Hat in the Pyms' Monteverdi, and Adam and I followed at a respectful distance in the Peugeot.

'Why is he giving us lunch?' asked Adam. 'Getting a drink out of the bastard is like getting a pork chop out of a rabbi.'

I was fairly mystified myself. Rodney did not, in my experience, buy anybody anything. He had the true meanness of the very rich, and was fond of saying, 'It's only the poor who buy everyone in sight a drink. The rich don't have to prove anything.' He said this with such conviction that people with a hundredth of his income, or no income at all, would frequently pay for his whisky, as if confronted by an unquestionable truth.

'It's his wedding anniversary,' I said, remembering. Their reception at the hotel had been my most profitable day last year.

'Of course,' said Adam, and his face broke into a huge, happy smile.

'Why does the memory of the Pyms' wedding bring on that expression?' I asked.

He paused for a while and then said, 'If I tell you something, keep it to yourself.'

'If I tell anybody it will be in strict confidence,' I assured him.

'I've kept it a secret for a year but I have a feeling it's safe to tell you now.'

I smelt a succulent piece of gossip heading my way.

'I always fancied Julie,' he said finally. 'But I never managed to meet her until he brought her into the Bali. By that time she had fallen in love with his bank balance and they were already engaged.'

'You make her sound a trifle mercenary,' I suggested.

'She had to think of her future,' he said forgivingly. 'Starving in a garret isn't the modern girl's style — there are too many new toys in the shops: video recorders, music centres, freezers, waste disposal units. Indispensable prerequisites for modern living, they tell me, although I have never owned any of them.'

The Monteverdi turned off the main road and we followed it down a much narrower country lane.

'So what happened?' I asked. I could sense that there was a piece of top quality gossip hovering here somewhere — I wanted to get my hands on it.

'She prefers me.'

I felt slightly short-changed at this; I was looking for something meatier.

'What leads you to that conclusion?' I asked in a tone of voice which suggested as clearly as possible that nothing had taken me in that direction.

'You may remember that Rodney held a stag party at your establishment at which I was not?'

'I recall the stag party. Your absence? No.'

'Well, it's always flattering to be missed,' said Adam. 'I was at home in my flat, being somewhat short of folding money.'

'It sounds like a boring evening.'

'It was the greatest evening of my life.'

'What happened?'

'Julie came round.'

'She did?'

'There was a knock on the door of my bijou pad. I opened it

93

and she walked straight in without a word. She turned round in the centre of the room, did something to a shoulder strap, and her dress fell round her ankles. She had nothing on underneath.'

'What did you say?' I asked, thinking of a few appropriate lines.

'I was speechless, but she wasn't. She said, "Tomorrow I am a married woman. Today I am not." '

'That's quite a long speech for Julie.'

'It was the last one she made for three hours.'

'What happened? Couldn't you lob in a few lewd details, just to flesh the story out?'

'I did everything to her that a man can do to a woman. By midnight she couldn't sit down and I couldn't stand up.'

'And the following day she staggered up the aisle.' I looked ahead at the pert co-star of this sexual extravaganza, but she was masked by Mrs Stapleton in the back seat of the Monteverdi. This was gossip of the very highest quality. But whom could I tell?

Then I remembered some other gossip.

'I've heard that Rodney is a bit odd,' I told Adam.

'In what way?'

'Sexually.'

I had heard somewhere from somebody — I can protect my source because I've forgotten it — that he found it necessary in the bedroom to devise ever more exotic dishes to stimulate his jaded appetite. In one inventive but apparently gratifying manoeuvre he dislocated his knee, but reappeared a day or two later, smiling but limping, feeling evidently that he had pushed back the frontiers on some ill-lit boundary of human knowledge.

'I always imagine Julie waiting for him back at home with whips, handcuffs, silk suspenders with studs down the side, German Army helmets, decorated cucumbers, plastic vibrators . . .'

Adam looked restless.

'You just missed a great opportunity to keep your mouth shut,' he said.

*   *   *

The Cloche Hat was in every good food guide. It was owned and run by an eccentric Czech who in ten years had created a gourmet's paradise from most unlikely beginnings. It was a dark wooden one-storey building with room for only twelve tables and a discreet bar in one corner. Oak pillars in the middle of the room gave the illusion of privacy for most of the tables, all of which were antique, but the Cloche Hat's reputation rested confidently on its food, not its unusual atmosphere. The clientele was predictable, for the place had cachet. There were a lot of rising stars in second-rate firms, dressed uniformly in bespoke lightweight suits and Gucci moccasins. They had hungry eyes and trendy moustaches and a prodigious talent for ingratiating themselves. Their women knocked your eye out — the better the restaurant, the more beautiful the women who eat in it.

At a table in one corner I could see the local Member of Parliament, who spent a large part of his professional life struggling to get some forlorn feminist demand on the statute book — free boxing gloves for battered wives, I think it was. The silicone-pumped, exquisitely coiffured but ageing partners of rich men, which the area abundantly possessed, crowded round the barman.

As Adam and I walked in, Rodney appeared carrying a tray bearing six glasses of champagne. I had thought we were five but Julie, I now noticed, was talking to a large, fat, balding man with ginger hair. Moving to one side — but scooping up my champagne first — I saw that we were in the presence of the legendary Chad Cartwright, whose story was *risqué*, too. Only a few weeks earlier the sudden reminder of it had led me to this profound human truth: A Man In Need Of Sexual Relief Is Capable Of Great Foolishness.

This insight arrived, complete with capital letters, while I was watching one of those provincial news bulletins that convulse viewers who don't receive their television programmes from London, and are treated nightly to some pofaced yob telling them that an allotment shed has caught fire, a dog has been run over or a shopper has been felled by a tin of beans, accidentally dislodged from the top shelf in a super-market.

On this night the big news was that a 'prominent citizen' in one of those tidy southern towns where men not only still wear hats but also raise them, had been discovered at midnight in a builder's yard with his trousers round his ankles and his secretary in close, even intimate, attendance. This, of course, isn't on its own an offence against English law, particularly if you are on drinking terms with the builder who owns the yard, but some violence involving the secretary's husband had followed and the whole story had been revealed that day to a presumably grateful court. I was certainly grateful — you can hear too much on my television about stamp-collecting traffic wardens and similar headline-grabbers.

Anyway, after I had turned off the set and was thinking about this merchant with the chilly knees in a damp builder's yard, I remembered Chad. The great truth that had just been revealed to me had, I realized, made itself known many years before. Chad was expelled from our school for having sexual relations with the cricket pavilion, and if you know of any greater foolishness than that, please don't tell me.

We were in the sixth form then and for many of us it was the start of our education. For ten or twelve years we had been bored rigid by sundry pedagogues chuntering on about scientific principles, historical facts, mathematical certainties, the abstruse and abstract notions of long-dead brain-pans, and suddenly we were trusted — released — to follow our own bent. One boy wrote a musical. Another designed a house. I read the whole of Dickens.

Many, admittedly, decided that their development could best be encouraged by five hours of football a day, with three pints of cider and a spot of shop-lifting at lunchtime, but Chad wandered off down a prurient path of his own. If it wasn't *Men Only* it was *Health and Efficiency*. His interests narrowed quickly and soon became marvellously concentrated. What was surprising was that nobody shared them: we must have been a retarded lot. Of course this was before the joys of comprehensive education, O-level gang bangs and the like; in those days we didn't even know what girls were for. Chad hung around with his salacious secrets, but nobody wanted to

96

share them. He received no sympathy at all from his former friends and eventually became something of a pariah. It seemed to unsettle him in some way and he became morose.

He was a big red-headed boy, the tallest in the class and probably — nobody ever weighed us — the heaviest. He had been the first eleven's centre forward and first wicket down in the cricket eleven. In fact, in the fifth year — this is a laugh — he won the *mens sana* prize, an award that subsequently reduced the headmaster to fury.

But all his interests faded away in the sixth year. The football boots were hung up, the cricket bat was stowed away and the games master was politely informed that he was 'no longer available' for selection. The only sporting appurtenance to survive in his affections, apparently, was the cricket pavilion.

He used to arrive at school in a screeching of brakes on a bright blue Vespa, being far too insensitive to notice that ostentation was ostracized at our seat of learning. His father was a self-taught plumber, which seemed to us then to be the thing to get into if your kids were going to skid around on a Vespa when the others struggled to school on second-hand bikes.

For some reason Chad devoted some of his boundless energy to befriending me (had I a wooden personality? A heart of oak?). I am what they call a good listener and the hours of boredom that this sociable virtue has cost me would stun a rhinoceros. What Chad liked to chat about was Chad, and if you told him that you had just been discussing things with Jesus Christ in the playground his eyes would glaze over until he got the conversation back to where it ought to be.

'I have some most reprehensible inhibitions,' he said one day, standing alongside the desk where I was ploughing through *Silas Marner*. Personally I didn't think there was much to choose between the problems of Silas and the problems of Chad, but I wanted to get the book finished — for ever — and I told him I'd see him later. He never returned to the subject and after he had left I was sorry that I had not encouraged a few revelations that day. It might have thrown some light on the cricket pavilion business.

The pavilion, when I used it, was an aesthetically displeasing edifice that you left in hope and re-entered almost immediately with excuses. But with Chad it was obviously the reverse.

It was a sinister black pinewood building, seven-inch ship-lap boarding, with many of the wood's knots necessarily missing. The scorer's box protruded from its sloping roof like a dormer window, and the pillars at the front, where future batsmen sat in deckchairs, had been painted white as a cheerful contrast to the rest of its creosoted gloominess. At one side a lean-to shed had been built on to house the roller that was hauled across the cricket table every morning as a prefect's punishment. And — without referring to its grimy interior, its dank atmosphere, its pungent odours — that is all I care to say about the pavilion.

A sex object? A provocation? A thing of beauty and a joy forever? A sight to render a healthy young man dizzy with lust? I think not. Chad, perhaps, would have paid tribute to its classical profile, its apparent unapproachability, its tantalizing air of detachment, but Chad never got a chance.

It was, like most winters in England, the worst in living memory, with ice, snow, fog and slush, but I didn't realize how bad it was until seagulls started squawking over my head, thirty miles inland. Because of the weather, the sports field and the pavilion were placed out of bounds lest two tons of wet mud were transferred by scores of tiny feet into the school's spotless classrooms.

The gymnasium, an ancient barn-like building that stood on its own across the playground, became the social centre for the more physical type of pupil and, bored with books, I wandered down there one morning to beat up a punchbag. Table tennis was the big craze that year, halitosis having killed off blow football, but others were boxing, jumping over things or hanging precariously from wall-bars.

In one corner, on his own, the former sportsman Chad was doing press-ups on his thumbs. Nearby was his inevitable collection of erotic reading matter and finally, as a welcome change from the classics, I picked one up and flipped through it.

'See nipples and die,' grunted Chad from the floor.

On the inside cover there was an advertisement for a sex manual. 'The caresses, positions and manoeuvres described in this book can make your marriage bed a constantly replenishing fount of vital satisfaction,' I read.

Chad jumped to his feet and came over.

'Losing a little surplus energy?' I asked, but that wasn't what he wanted the conversation to be about.

'Do you think that sex shortens a man's life?' he asked. 'I can't help noticing that the Popes go on for ever.'

'Apparently not,' I replied. 'Married men live longer than bachelors.'

'What's that got to do with it?' Chad said. 'It's the single men who are getting the most sex, isn't it?'

Not knowing the answers to this problem I drifted off and found some boxing gloves. Around me dozens of pubescent youths, who bravely imagined that a place on an Olympic winner's rostrum was reserved for them, prepared for sporting glory. The fact that without exception they were going to wind up with the same personality-crushing jobs, pale faces and shiny trousers as everybody else had obviously not occurred to their hopeful minds.

Chad watched me hitting the punchbag for a few minutes and then he picked up his magazines and wandered off.

That lunchtime, oblivious of the cloying mud and the driving sleet, he deflowered the cricket pavilion.

Unfortunately, he was also oblivious of Wheezing Beasley, the geography master, who was on lunchtime duty patrolling the sports field to ensure that the out-of-bounds notices were being obeyed. They said afterwards, although this could be part of the legend, that it was the rhythmic rocking of the pavilion railings which had first alerted Beasley's foggy mind.

That afternoon we were corralled into one of the occasional lessons that were provided for the sixth formers to remind them that they were still at school and not yet entirely free. This one was given by an insane music teacher who had recently discovered religion and who consequently marched round the building smiling, his head spinning with bizarre ideas. Not knowing a solo cantata from an instrumental concerto I was defeating boredom with a paperback under the desk ('So there could be no doubt that Wilhelm Storitz was implicated').

The music man had been rambling incoherently for less than ten minutes when the door burst open and a red-faced headmaster strode in. He was a malevolent little bastard who in today's liberal climate would, quite rightly, have his teeth kicked down his throat by bored and disillusioned pupils. He was a vain dwarf with one of those absurdly low partings which tell you that hairless acres are being concealed around here somewhere.

His entrance was extraordinary: usually he knocked. It soon emerged that his purpose today was to pour some valedictory abuse over Chad.

'Cartwright!' he shouted. 'Stand up.'

Chad stood up. You could tell that he knew what was coming, but the rest of us were curious — curious and fascinated. We were not aware at that stage that the cricket pavilion now had a different look in its eye.

'In 1642,' said the headmaster, speaking very slowly, 'this country produced Isaac Newton. Now it produces you.' We looked at the headmaster and we looked at Chad. I was so enthralled that I would probably have looked round for Isaac Newton as well had the headmaster not suddenly shouted, 'YOU'VE GOT THE MORALS OF A RACOON!'

In the face of this rudeness Chad maintained a cool silence. He was too old and too big to be alarmed by the lunatics from the staff-room, but his silence spelt guilt to the rest of us. If he had a case he would now be presenting it.

The headmaster walked down the aisle between the desks until he came to Chad. For one glorious moment the possibility of unbridled violence simmered before us, but when they were side by side the head found himself looking up ten or twelve inches to meet Chad's unwavering gaze and, instead, he said, 'Come with me, lad!'

100

He turned and marched dramatically from the room. Chad followed him nonchalantly, throwing V-signs at his departing back.

That was the last time we saw him and nothing else happened except that, hilariously enough, Beasley asked to be relieved of lunchtime duties patrolling the sports field. He probably couldn't face the long years of anti-climax that lay ahead.

It would be nice to report that Chad's departure was followed by a suitably sombre mood, a wave of regret among the friends whom he had so abruptly abandoned. Serious reflections on a man ruined, a career destroyed, would have seemed an appropriate sequel to this awful episode.

Boys being boys, however, the truth is that his dismissal was followed by a spate of Chad jokes that rocked the school for months and probably years. There was a new one every day while I was still there — he had given his girlfriend Dutch elm disease, he had become the proud father of a dog kennel. There were even those who swore that his indiscriminate sexual tastes had aroused the interest of an alert publisher, who had commissioned him to write his story. The title, they said, was going to be *Take The Sack Off Its Head, I Want To Kiss It*.

Chad himself became known in his absence as Chad The Impaler. It wouldn't surprise me at all to discover that the witty line you hear so often today, 'a legend in his own lunchtime', hadn't originated with his downfall and disgrace on that winter afternoon.

Thinking about all this late that evening a few months ago, I suddenly realized why the midnight episode in the builder's yard had set me thinking about Chad, who, after all, was a character from the distant past. I had enlivened, or grounded, a few sagging conversations over the years with the story of his memorable exploit but, mostly, I hadn't given him much thought since he left school.

I hurled myself across the room, put the television back on and changed channels, all in one dextrous manoeuvre.

'The girls are stripping off,' said a male voice that was

managing to stay remarkably calm in the circumstances. I waited impatiently for the picture to catch up with the sound. When it did, four athletes of uncertain gender were slumped over their starting blocks on a running track. I stayed with the sport, despite the crassness of the commentary, because this channel, too, liked to round off its evening with a soporific summary of the local trivia.

And then — when the girls had run and the men had jumped and a cross between the two had thrown things — there he was: Chad Cartwright, red hair receding above a much fatter face than I had known, a heaviness around the eyes, a neat military moustache, a double chin. I had obviously heard his name on the earlier bulletin and it had made me remember him without realizing that he was the man in the story. He was the former mayor and now, under local government reorganization, the chairman of a council that administered a much larger area. By profession he was a property developer, and as the cameras filmed him hurrying from the court he slid into a £30,000 Aston Martin at the kerb and drove quickly away. He might still be at the mercy of an aberrant libido, but he was doing a lot better than his father, the self-taught plumber.

The court had cleared him of the charge of assaulting his secretary's husband and upheld his plea of self-defence. The incident in the builder's yard had been misunderstood, he told the court, but the television reporter didn't tell us what Chad's version was. Perhaps he was doing press-ups on his thumbs.

A spokesman for the council said that the matter was closed and denied angrily that the day's events would have any effect on Mr Cartwright's career in local government, and then the news bulletin hurried on to other more edifying topics: a telephone kiosk had been vandalized, a village post office robbed.

At first I was surprised to see Chad standing in the Cloche Hat, but then I remembered that his host was a property developer as well and, with the fortuitous bonus of Chad's council position, clandestine deals between this twosome could pour thousands of pounds into both their bank accounts while ratepayers winced under the bill.

'I saw that man on television the other day,' said Adam.

'He's Chad The Impaler,' I said, and went over to him.

'You know what they say,' he was telling Rodney. 'A million here, a million there, and soon you're talking about real money. Good God, it's Martin Lomax!'

He held out his hand to me.

'Hallo, Chad. How's your television career coming along?'

'The less said about that the better,' he replied. 'What are you doing? It must be twenty years . . .'

'More than that. I own a small hotel down the road.'

'Which one?'

'The Bali.'

'I know it. I'll give you three hundred thousand pounds for it. I've always wanted to own a hotel.'

'Really?'

It had cost my parents about £40,000 a long time ago. Of course there had been some improvements.

'Give me first option if you ever want to sell. I may even up the offer.'

'I'll remember. What are you doing here?'

'Rodney and I are in the same game.' He turned very slightly to the others to indicate that further questions on the subject would not be welcome.

'You own property all over the place, I suppose?' I said. I can ignore a hint as well as take it.

'Quite a lot,' he agreed, nodding.

'Got many cricket pavilions?'

It jolted him a little.

'I hope you are not one of those boring people who live in the past?' he said.

'I can't remember the day before yesterday,' I promised.

He winked what I took to be a thank-you, and slipped his arm round Julie's shoulder. Her face had that natural look which takes two hours to achieve; it gave me her usual wary smile, which after the journey here I finally understood. Today I was the eager custodian of everybody's guilty secrets.

'Shall we go to our table?' said our leader, looking for somewhere to dump his tray.

'Yes, let's,' said Mrs Stapleton. 'It's only the English who think that eating and drinking are two quite separate activities.' She turned to me and whispered, 'It's a long time since anybody bought me a meal!'

A table for six was ready by a window. Rodney sat at one end and Julie at the other. I sat next to Adam and Mrs Stapleton and Chad faced us.

'Martin and I were at school together,' Chad announced. 'What a bloody farce that was. My education began the day I left.'

'Scottish education is much superior,' said Mrs Stapleton. 'My husband was Scottish.'

'What about America?' said Chad. 'You watch their trade unionists or sports stars being interviewed on television. Their opposite numbers here can't string two words together, but that lot are more articulate than the Prime Minister.'

As we contemplated this humiliation a waiter appeared from nowhere with six enormous menus. So far, I noticed, Adam's and Julie's eyes had not met. She studied the menu now and announced that she would have a salad as she was slimming.

'Half the world is slimming and the other half starving,' said Mrs Stapleton. 'Did you know that during the month of Ramadan food consumption actually increases in Arab countries because people get so hungry during the day?'

I ordered fillet of steak 'cooked in butter with herbs and garlic, served on a bed of creamed spinach flavoured with nutmeg'. It sounded interesting. Back at the Bali it would probably have been braised steak and toothpicks. I finished the champagne and looked round for more but Rodney was ordering wine.

Chad produced a small cigar in anticipation of the long wait which class restaurants regard as proper and stared across at Adam as if he had only just noticed him.

'What do you do?' he asked. He was wearing an expensive sporty suit in brown check, he had ordered quails' breasts in aspic as if he had it every day, and he looked very successful.

'At the moment?' said Adam. 'Nothing.'

'In the past? In the future?' asked Chad.

'Adam is a very nice man but he is not very successful,' said Mrs Stapleton. 'The world beats a path past his door.'

'I am surrounded by capitalists,' said Adam, smiling. 'I am not one.'

'Capitalism has one immeasurable advantage over the other system,' said Chad. 'The police don't pay social calls in the middle of the night. I rather appreciate that, being a bit partial to my snooze.'

'Oh, I've got nothing against it,' said Adam. 'How do you join?'

'His life is one long quest for a money-making idea,' I said.

'Good,' said Chad. 'Keep it simple, that's the motto. You want something that costs threepence to make, ten pence to sell and is bought by millions every year. A can opener, something like that.'

'I'll work on it,' said Adam.

'If you come up with something and need capital come to me,' Chad said. 'Everything I touch turns to gold.'

'Everything I touch turns to sawdust,' said Adam.

Food arrived eventually in the company of a man sporting a red bow tie. Outside, the weather forecasters had got it right for once: the rain was beating down.

Chad ate greedily in response to the demands of his huge frame. ('I've given up jogging,' he told us. 'It interfered with the university seismograph.') Adam ate fastidiously, as if unused to such treats, and I was a fairly picky eater myself. Gorging offended some residual social conscience. Drinking left no guilt at all: a third of the world weren't thirsty.

It was only after Rodney had drunk a few glasses of wine himself that the reason for his invitation became apparent. What he had in mind was a public denunciation of Adam, who was to be lectured, chastised and dismissed. However, Adam was much too straightforward to be vulnerable to the sort of bullying that Rodney planned.

When the eating had finished and the plates had been collected, our host sat back as if he was the chairman of a high-powered board meeting.

'I have invited you here today,' he announced, 'because Julie and I are celebrating our first wedding anniversary.'

Nobody seemed quite able to summon up an appropriate retort to this: the private lives of your friends are best discussed in their absence. I raised my glass.

'A toast to you both,' I suggested.

'I have always thought that marriage is like living in an open prison,' said Chad, when we had all drunk to the benefactors of the feast. 'But good luck to you.'

'Are you married at the moment?' I asked, remembering the court case on television.

'I've been married three times, but I'm not at the moment,' he said. He reached over for a bottle of wine and filled his glass. 'I shall marry again if I can find the right woman. It took me ages to work out why my last wife would never make love with the light on.'

'And why was it?' asked Mrs Stapleton.

'She couldn't bear to see me enjoying myself.'

This theory cast a slight pall over what was meant to be a celebration of the matrimonial institution and Rodney, flushed now with wine, began to look agitated at the end of the table.

'Well, I like marriage,' he said. 'I wanted it, I got it and I like it.' He turned towards Adam, the colour draining miraculously from his face. 'What about you, Adam?'

'I agree,' he said. 'I'm looking for a wife myself.'

'And you don't mind whose?' Rodney slammed back.

The unexpected turn in the conversation plunged us all into an embarrassed silence.

'I do,' said Adam eventually. 'I'm very fussy. But, given a choice, I'd prefer yours.'

'Ah!' said Rodney, triumphantly. 'You admit it that readily!'

I could tell from the changing patterns on Julie's forehead that this conversation was a strain to her.

'You see,' Rodney went on, 'that's why I invited you here. To sort it out.' His old-fashioned spectacles were in danger of steaming up as he waved an arm about and addressed us all.

'This gentleman,' he said, 'this *guest* of mine telephoned my beloved wife in the middle of the night demanding sex.'

'Did he get any?' asked Mrs Stapleton. I realized from her gaze that the wine had hit her, too.

'Don't be a damn fool, Mrs Stapleton,' said Rodney. 'This is serious.'

'It's disgraceful,' said Chad, slipping without a blush into the role of moral guardian. If Adam had been prowling around with a bottle of unguent in search of a promiscuous cricket pavilion Chad would presumably have been buying him drinks.

For a moment I was tempted to try to defuse an explosive situation, imagining that these familiar sounds of a row were taking place on my own premises. It was with relief that I sat back to enjoy it.

'Your beloved wife!' said Adam, very calmly. 'Whom you punch, abuse and despise.'

Rodney had become very agitated now, moving round quickly on his seat as if there was somebody underneath jabbing a skewer through it.

Julie stirred at last, stretching a tremulous arm in front of me to restrain Adam. Their hands met, romantically or otherwise, across a crowded ashtray.

'Don't, Adam,' she said.

Rodney stared at him and then her. 'Tell them it's not true,' he said. His eyes pleaded for obedience.

Adam was calmly probing his teeth with a matchstick in search of undigested morsels.

'Tell them it's not true,' he said, 'or he'll beat you up again.'

'I never hit women myself,' said Chad quickly, trying to inject some normality into the conversation. 'You feel so bad about it afterwards.'

'How do you know you feel bad about it afterwards,' asked Mrs Stapleton, 'if you never hit them?'

This conundrum remained unsolved, however, for Rodney, demolished by Julie's silence, climbed unsteadily to his feet and declared wanly, 'I've had enough of this. You can pay for the bloody meal yourselves.'

He marched out into the rain.

'I'm not surprised,' said Mrs Stapleton, pulling her purse from her bag. 'That bugger never bought anybody anything.'

'No, I'll pay,' said Chad, producing a plastic chain of credit cards more than a foot long. 'I'm sure he'll reimburse me when he calms down.'

Nobody raised any objection to this suggestion and Chad beckoned a waiter.

In the silence we could all hear Julie sobbing: it was the most noise she had made all day.

I discovered Catchpole's little secret when I got back to the hotel. Before falling wearily into bed the previous evening I had dumped his pack of cards by the side of my bed and not noticed them when I crawled, eyes half open, into the bathroom that morning.

They stood out now, though, and I picked them up and examined them because there was something familiar about their appearance. They were a Mocker deck, just like the ones I had received years ago in my Christmas stocking. A Mocker deck is used by boys for card tricks: they have a floral design on the back and the petals are marked.

For ammunition like this to fall into my hands made me wonder if God wasn't up there after all — no beleaguered garrison ever received the cavalry's arrival with such pleasure. I hastened downstairs with my news.

Catchpole lay on his back on the floor, wide awake, as if he were passing the time by counting to two million.

'I have some good news and some bad news,' I told him.

He didn't move. 'Give me the good news,' he said.

'I've found your pack of cards.'

He didn't say anything.

'Don't you want the bad news?'

He still didn't say anything. He lay on his back and didn't even look at me.

'I don't think your friends are going to be all that delighted with the way you've been cheating them.'

Two large hands came up from the floor and completely covered his face, but no sound emerged.

'You've been conning them for months, taking all their money, pretending to be their friend.'

No reply arrived and I went up to the bars to see his reaction, but his face was still covered by two huge hands.

'And they think that you're a brilliant poker player,' I said. 'They must be pretty thick if you can beat them week in and week out with a Mocker deck.'

He didn't answer this either, and I waited a long time for him to speak next.

'Please,' he said. 'Don't tell them.'

'So that you can carry on stealing their money?'

'Burn the deck.'

'You'll buy another.'

He finally removed his hands and sat up on the floor.

'I'll do a deal with you. A hundred pounds. Two hundred. Five hundred?'

'You'd win that back in no time, Edwin.'

'I'll leave here without any trouble.'

But I had already solved the problem of getting him out of the cell, and I didn't trust him anyway.

'I think your friends deserve to be told,' I said. 'That way you won't have any friends.'

'Please, Lomax,' he said pleadingly. His harsh voice quavered, and his pale face was the colour of snow.

'*Mr* Lomax, corporal,' I said. 'And stand up when you talk to me.'

Surprisingly, he stood up. It wasn't that he lacked a sense of humour — although he did; he would probably have stood on his head if I had asked him.

'I'll do anything you want,' he said, to confirm this. 'Just don't tell them.'

'I'll tell them, Catchpole,' I said. 'You can bet your ill-gotten winnings on that.'

He put his head in his hands again.

'I won't be able to go home,' he said pathetically.

'Home?' I said. 'Who said you're going home?'

8

Are women's breasts getting bigger or is it something I have eaten? The thought occurred to me that afternoon when Laurel stepped out of a taxi into the rain. She was wearing a yellow T-shirt which bore the mysterious legend 'The Diving Centre of Estepona'.

I was thirty-six when women stopped looking at me in the street. At first I thought that some temporary eye complaint was afflicting eager husband-seekers, a judgement I rescinded on consulting a mirror. An even more traumatic milestone occurred a year later when a former girlfriend of mine — an erotic little bundle during our turbulent relationship — became a grandmother. I went into the kitchen at the Bali and made cocoa, feeling like a man who had missed both shows and the champagne party afterwards. The years had slipped past at varying speeds. Now I was thirty-eight, a statistic that filled me with the foreboding which was no doubt responsible for the rapturous reception I gave Laurel. Sex appeal, like oil, is a finite resource.

I lifted her off her feet and kissed her in mid-air.

'Wow,' she said. 'Also gosh!'

I ignored the rain that was soaking us and kissed her again. For a girl from the city where a troglodyte's pallor is almost *de rigueur*, she was attractively tanned.

'You're the most welcome guest this year,' I said, taking both her hands. 'Probably last year as well.'

'Does that mean I have to pay?' she asked, pulling away and laughing.

111

'No, but you might have to work. The chef's taking tomorrow off.'

'What fun! I'll give you a menu to remember.'

Her blue suitcases stood on the step and I picked them both up.

'Let me show you to our room, ma'am,' I said.

'Separation is amputation, honey,' trilled Laurel in some southern American accent.

Establishing her in my bedroom was the work of minutes; her takeover of my private bathroom was a major event. Mysterious bottles were pulled from dainty Italian bags and crammed on to the shelves beside the wash bowl: creams, perfumes, oils and baby powder; bath oil, talcum powder, body lotion, Estée Lauder daily moisture supply, antiperspirant and something called 'creamy milk cleanser'. Almay non-oily eye make-up remover was followed by Scholl foot cream, cotton wool and tissues. There was no room to empty the toilet bag with its mascara and eye shadow and lipstick and blusher — the place was full of jars fragrant with musk, and make-up sticks that disguise sleepless nights, remove blotches, eradicate spots, reassure users and mislead innocent bachelor observers. Of course, when Napoleon sent Josephine a message saying 'Back in three days — don't wash' the multi-million dollar cosmetic industry hadn't really taken off.

I was spotlessly clean myself, anxiously prepared for whatever sexual olympics were coming my way. But even with my faith in lettuce I didn't expect to equal the Bali Hotel sexual record, which had been set that year by a brawny Arab who arrived one Friday evening for 'two days of love', as he called it, with a lady from Brighton, and who vanished with her into room three for forty-eight hours. He came down to the bar alone on the Sunday evening, looking marginally less brawny, and asked for a beer.

'How was the weekend of love?' I asked him. I always liked to show an interest in my customers' activities.

'Very good,' he said in perfect English. 'She had seventy-five orgasms and I had fifteen.'

112

The reply, somewhat franker than I had expected or even wanted, stunned me for a moment. Eventually I asked, 'Are you sure?'

'Of course I am sure. We kept the score with chalk marks on the bedstead.'

Later, when I went up, as it were, to fumigate the room, I found that he was telling the truth. There were seventy-five chalk lines on one side of the bed and fifteen on the other. I didn't know whether to remove them or photograph them.

However, today's guest had other plans. She flung open the bedroom window and stared out at the rain.

'I was hoping for a boat on the river,' she said. 'I'd forgotten about the English summer.'

'Perhaps tomorrow,' I said. 'In the meantime we're house-bound. What's on television?'

I had no intention of watching television but if two people start to watch it from the depths of a double bed it can get to be quite cosy.

'A film,' she said, reading from my newspaper. 'A sensitive and imaginative example of the new Australian cinema, exploring the fantasy world of a spinster who finds herself alone after the death of the bedridden mother she has nursed for years.'

'Poor spinster,' I said, hinting ineptly at the weekend's main business.

'I've seen a dozen different versions of that story,' said Laurel. 'She gets religion in the end and commits suicide. Let's go make a cup of tea.'

We went downstairs, hand in hand. The hotel was deserted.

'I thought you told me the Bali is where it is at,' said Laurel. 'It looks as if the Bali is where it has been.'

I led her into the kitchen and made tea.

'What is to be for you?' I asked. 'Spinsterhood, religion and suicide?'

'Marriage — stardust or sawdust?' she replied. 'The pub-licity it gets is awful. My brother got married last year and it didn't encourage me at all. The service was short and the marriage didn't last much longer.'

'What happened to it?'

'It broke down and then it broke up. He said he only got married to go to wife-swapping parties and then he found that nobody else wanted her.'

'Young people are so cynical today.'

'She was a bit neurotic. When he went out for a drink she would wait a while and then sneak down after him to see what he was up to.'

'That's friendly.'

'He fixed her, though. He used to turn the clocks back two hours before he left the house.'

She dunked a Turkish Delight in her tea. She did not have the normal awful female talent for going on talking long after she had ceased to have anything to say.

'I didn't know you had a brother,' I said.

'I had two. Now I have one.'

'What happened to the other one?'

'You wouldn't believe me if I told you.'

'I'd like to hear it, though.' Getting her to talk about her family was a trusted method of bringing a girl closer to you. I fetched some cakes and Laurel took two.

'Timothy was the brainy one, the youngest of the three of us. He was studying sociology at a university up north. He had a brilliant mind — brilliant and much, much too complicated. One night four years ago he threw his books into his Mini and drove home, no one knows why. We were all asleep and didn't hear him come in. First, evidently, he drank an entire bottle of Vodka. Then he dismantled the grandfather clock. He filled his pockets with the pieces and left the house. Nobody knows where he went but at four o'clock two police cars that had received messages about a bright red Mini that was being driven dangerously through Buckinghamshire and Oxford converged on Stratford and trapped Timothy's car on a bridge over the river.'

She drank some tea and examined her cake before finishing her story.

'To avoid the police he jumped from the bridge. He was a

114

reasonable swimmer but weighted down by the remains of the grandfather clock he sank like a brick.'

'What an extraordinary tale,' I said.

'He was an extraordinary boy.'

We sat in the kitchen eating our cakes. The story, true or false, had created a mood that was deeply unhelpful to my plans, but her next remark renewed my evanescent hopes.

'I thought you should know about our family,' she said. 'We're probably all nuts.'

'You look perfect to me.'

She smiled at last. 'No visible scars. Never raced or rallied. Look — do you run to clothes by Yves St Laurent, Cartier wedding rings and Gucci shoes?'

'Nothing less will do,' I said, and leaned over the table to kiss her. We were interrupted at this crucial moment by the tinkling of the bell on the reception desk. I walked out through the empty restaurant, wondering what commitment had just been sealed in the kitchen.

The man with his hand on the bell in reception was Adam, rainswept, windswept, and generally looking as if the hounds of hell were at his heels.

'I want a favour, pal,' he said urgently.

'A friend in need is a friend to be avoided,' I said pleasantly.

'I want a double room for a couple of nights.'

'That's not a favour. That's welcome business.'

'I have no money.'

'Ah.'

'I'll pay you eventually.'

'You want some standby credit?' I said. 'Why do you need a double room?'

'I have Julie outside. She's going to leave that rat. If I take her to my place he'll kick the door in and I'll get thrown out.'

'What about my doors?' I asked.

'He won't know we're here.'

'Ah,' I repeated.

I studied the book on the reception desk and found him the keys for room ten.

'A lovely view of the river, sir,' I said.

He was too distracted even to thank me and hurried back to the main door to beckon to Julie, who was outside. She looked windswept, too.

'The wind went right through me,' she said.

'Lucky old wind,' I joked, but Adam didn't smile and I realized that Julie had been accorded a new status now and was not a fit subject for such humour.

'Room ten,' said Adam, waving the key in front of her like a man who had just taken the top two floors of the Paris Sheraton.

Mrs Pym, with the minimal luggage of a bolting spouse, headed guiltily for the stairs.

'What now?' I said to Adam when she had gone. 'A bit of horizontal jogging, I suppose.'

'You've got a kind nature but a nasty mouth,' he said, picking up a battered hold-all which I now saw he had brought with him.

'My goodness,' I said. 'You are taking this seriously. Do you think she's going to stay with you? I mean, don't build up your hopes.'

'She wanted me all along,' Adam declared.

'What happened?' I asked. 'He confuse her with his wallet?'

'It was my fault. I didn't have the confidence to go in strongly enough. It's all going to be different now.' He held up his hand in a farewell gesture, as if he was embarking on a long journey.

'Be good,' I said. 'If you can't be good, be good at it.'

He smiled gratefully and disappeared. I made a note that the room was now occupied and wondered how long I would have to wait for payment.

If I am nice to somebody today, will somebody be nice to me tomorrow?

A man who owns a hotel is always misunderstood. The public sees him in the bar, often enough with a glass in his hand, and secretly hates him for the congenial and easy life that they imagine he is leading. The real work that he does is the nine-

116

tenths of the iceberg that the public doesn't see: the Sargasso Sea of paperwork involving staff, residents, suppliers, tax collectors and health inspectors; the physical work moving barrels, gas cylinders, crates, tanks, cartons of food, damaged furniture, faulty television sets and dustbins crammed with the constant flow of garbage. There is other physical work. I burn on average three beds every two years, thanks to the secret incontinence of my charming guests. I am an unpaid lavatory cleaner. I toil with water pipes, gas pipes, beer pipes. I clean the parts that a chambermaid cannot reach. I am a gardener.

The bubbles of satisfaction in this penal servitude are easily remembered and one of them accounted for Adam's cashless presence in room ten. He knew that I owed him a big favour.

Among the priceless goodies in my cellar (fine wines, spirits, one sausage salesman) is the world's cheapest collection of fruit juices, bitter lemons and tonics. I have enough of these dainty little bottles, which people love to empty into their gins and vodkas, to last the Bali Hotel for years, and they cost me nothing.

A few years ago the experts who justify their research fees by coming up with ever more bizarre conclusions, announced that these bottles contained a cancer-inducing ingredient. It was just after another collection of experts had announced that heart attacks were not only caused by smoking, butter, sudden exercise and sugar, but also by changes in the weather and fluctuations in the earth's magnetic field, and I was in no mood to take them seriously.

When Adam told me one evening that millions of bottles of this much valued adjunct to sociable drinking were being dumped each night by the manufacturers in a huge reservoir not twenty miles away, we both knew what we had to do. The wire netting which Adam produced had a one-inch mesh, like the wire netting on the front of a rabbit hutch. That night we drove out to the reservoir in my Peugeot and spent two hours laying the netting ten feet below the surface of the water. When it was firm we drove away and parked under some trees on a common and waited.

It was over an hour before we saw anybody, and Adam became restless.

'There's always a chance that they dumped the last lot yesterday,' he said.

'It was worth a try,' I told him. I found some music on the radio and looked at my watch: it was nearly midnight. A couple appeared from the woods behind us and walked down towards the road. It was a powerful lust, I thought, that sought gratification in these bleak surroundings.

At half-past twelve an enormous lorry appeared, and then another. I won't mention the well-known name on the side of these lorries — they could come looking for me. As the first one reversed to the edge of the water and prepared to disgorge its load, a third lorry appeared and then a fourth.

'We just struck gold,' I told Adam.

'I hope they won't come and ask what we're doing here,' he said.

'It's all right. We'll just hold hands.'

'If it's all the same to you, I'd sooner be arrested.'

By one o'clock the lorries had gone and we drove back to the reservoir.

When you live in the silence of the country it is difficult to judge the nearness of a sound. The car that you thought was arriving is pulling up two hundred yards away, and the human voice that you believed was addressing you is a man in conversation on the other side of a field. The slightest sound that night made us both nervous, but we realized afterwards that nobody had come within a quarter of a mile of our plunder.

Of course many of the boxes of drinks had missed our safety net, but we retrieved enough to fill the Peugeot six times.

We sped back to the Bali in the dark and unloaded the car in the yard at the rear. There was no time to take the booty indoors. We were racing against the arrival of the dawn and it was certainly the most exhausting night's work that either of us have ever undertaken. It was while we were cramming the car to the roof for the sixth time that we realized with some surprise that it was already light, and that we were about to

118

present a strange and suspicious sight to postmen, newsboys, milkmen and others who start their day's work when most people are still enjoying the night's big dream. We didn't skimp the job, though. The sixth load was as heavy as the first.

The stacked cartons behind the Bali Hotel obliterated the light from two rooms, and yet we had left behind as much as we had taken, resting below the surface on our wire netting. This sad fact meant that we were unable to reclaim the wire netting, which seemed to worry Adam.

'I only borrowed it,' he said. 'It must be worth twenty pounds.'

I gave him twenty pounds. 'And if you ever switch to bitter lemon at the Bali, it's on the house,' I told him.

'Most of it is on the bloody wire netting. Should we come back tomorrow?'

I started the engine. 'Are you mad? I'm never coming near this place again.' We had a final nervous look round for witnesses and then cruised off to the joyful sound of the birds' dawn chorus.

At the hotel Adam helped me transfer the cartons to the cellar. We moved quickly and quietly and had shifted the lot before the first insomniac guest came looking for an early breakfast.

Luckily it was one of Scott's rare days off and I was cooking breakfast that morning. I gave the first one to Adam, but I never did find out whether he reimbursed the owner of the wire netting.

Even the atheists who use my hotel do not expect the bar to open early on Sunday evenings, and I was sitting at the reception desk, reading a paper and waiting for Laurel, who was taking a shower upstairs, to join me for dinner, when the soap opera star, Gordon Hammerdale, appeared.

'I'm looking for someone,' he said flatly.

'Aren't we all?' I replied sweetly.

He missed this pleasantry, and announced, 'Edwin Catchpole's gone missing.'

'Would he be the gentleman in room seven?' I asked, gazing

down at the papers in front of me as if the information lay there somewhere.

'That's him,' said Gordon Hammerdale.

'I was going to tell you about that when you came in,' I said. 'Did you enjoy your golf, by the way?'

'What — in this bloody rain?' he snarled.

'There's always the nineteenth hole,' I said, with my best smile. 'Now, about Mr Catchpole. My chambermaid tells me that he didn't sleep in his room last night.'

'And we haven't seen him all day. Where the hell is he?'

'What has usually happened in this situation is that the gentleman has met a local girl,' I said. 'They can't bring them back here because it costs extra money, so they usually wind up spending most of their time at the girl's place.'

'Not Catchpole,' said Gordon Hammerdale. 'He doesn't chase girls. Anyway, he was getting drunk in the bar here last night.'

'I remember,' I said, remembering. 'But I didn't notice at the end of the evening whether he went upstairs or out.'

'His bed wasn't slept in?'

'Apparently not.'

Gordon Hammerdale looked confused, 'What's to be done?' he asked.

'Nothing,' I said firmly. 'He's a grown man and doesn't have to account to us for his movements. On the other hand, his room has got to be paid for, so he'd better show up soon. I can't let it to anyone else — his stuff is still in it.'

'Is it?' said Gordon Hammerdale. 'He's coming back then.'

'I'm sure he'll be here tomorrow,' I said confidently.

'Unless anything has happened to him.'

'Happened?'

'He could have had an accident. Do you think we should notify the police?'

It was difficult for me to convey, without arousing his suspicions, what a preposterous suggestion I thought this was, but I think I managed it.

'They'd laugh in your face,' I said. 'But perhaps we should consider it if he hasn't shown up by tomorrow.'

Gordon Hammerdale nodded solemnly. He had a personality, I thought, that was ideally suited to the attending of funerals. 'He's terrible with drink, you see. He could have wandered off and fallen asleep anywhere. But surely he would have woken up and come back by now.'

'I don't think he can have fallen asleep anywhere,' I said.

Gordon Hammerdale seemed reassured.

'Well, thanks. His pals said I ought to come and see you.'

He turned and went, leaving me to my newspaper. It was the first chance I had had to look at it today. I hadn't missed a lot: muggings, demos, industrial anarchy. Prices up, production down. Brains flying out, brawn rowing in, with forged passports. There was, an MP had revealed, an intractable malaise in the British nation. I had come through the other side of reading all that stuff and found nowadays that newspapers tended to create in me a frenzy of apathy.

I was putting the paper firmly to one side when Gordon Hammerdale reappeared.

'The bar's shut,' he said. For Gordon Hammerdale, it seemed to be one thing after another.

'Would you like it open?' I asked. On balance, I felt I should keep in with this man.

I got up and went out to the kitchen to fill the ice bucket. I took it through to the deserted bar, turned on the lights and removed the shutters. I didn't bother to open the doors that led on to the patio: nobody would be sitting outside tonight.

'I'll have a Bells,' said my only customer, 'and a Geneva panatella.'

I had lately taken to filling empty moments by whistling 'Abide With Me', which I took to be a bad sign. I went over to the juke box and put some lively music on, in case I started up again. From the front window I watched rain bouncing a foot off the car park. The sky was slate-grey from one horizon to the other.

As soon as Moaner Lisa arrived I would be able to visit the guest in the dungeon and surprise him with my generous gift of Scotch. By dawn he would be unconscious and back in his room and after that it would simply be a matter of keeping my nerve and wearing my poker face. Adam's fortuitous arrival, it occurred to me, was a lucky break because I could enlist his help in shifting the comatose Catchpole and rely on his silence.

I watched a car pull up in the car park and two men get out. They came into the bar. One of them had left his jacket in the car, despite the rain, and was sporting yellow braces. You have to be fundamentally insensitive to go around showing your braces, I told myself.

I crossed to the bar to serve them.

'So there you are,' said the first man. 'If you argue with them they lock you up and stick needles in you so that you don't want to sleep with women anymore.'

I thought for one distracted moment that our right-wing local council had adopted a new, more forceful attitude to querulous ratepayers, but the other man replied, 'Well, there's a moral to the story. Don't go to the Argentine if you're interested in politics.'

I served them beers as Lisa arrived.

'I'm sorry I'm late,' she said. 'I got caught in the rain.'

'Don't worry,' I told her. 'Look, my lady friend has come to stay so I might not be behind the bar too much tonight.'

'That's all right,' Lisa said, smiling. 'It's time you got married.'

'Who said anything about getting married?'

'I just did.'

I left her and made my way to the kitchen. Scott was preparing a sauce for the steaks.

'Okay for tomorrow?' he asked.

'Yes, but for God's sake don't break your leg.'

'I'm not taking part. I'm watching.'

I went over to the bread cupboard and began to make some cheese sandwiches. It seemed just the food to accompany a bottle of Scotch.

'Who are they for?' Scott asked.

'A customer in the bar.'

'Bit thick, aren't they?'

'He asked for them that way.'

122

I made three rounds and then decided to add onion. I stole some ready-washed lettuce that was intended for the prawn cocktails and put that in too. To round it off I found a Harrods Food Hall's bag that had been left in the kitchen and piled the sandwiches in it.

'You're not taking them out in a Harrods bag?' Scott asked.

'I am,' I said. 'You've got to impress the customers.'

9

My ursine buddy in the hoosegow looked as if he was beginning to suspect that his dismembered body would eventually be discovered in three plastic sacks. The cellar smelt like an otter's holt. Fifteen hours of solitary confinement had brought a curiously opaline complexion to his flabby features, which were composed firmly now in an expression of defeat. I was this side of exultant myself. He was sitting in the far corner of the cell and he didn't move when I came in. Catatonia had arrived. I imagined that his brute force and his golfer's energy had been sadly affected by nearly twenty-four hours without food, and I soon learned that it was food rather than freedom which was now obsessing him.

'If I was in Wormwood Scrubs at least they'd give me something to eat,' he said.

'True,' I replied. 'But look on the bright side. At least you're not getting buggered by an eight-foot guardsman every half-hour.'

'Have you seen my mates?' he asked.

'They found your pack of cards very interesting.'

The dismay that appeared on his face vanished just as quickly. 'Then you must have told them where I am? They know you've seen me!'

I shook my head. 'I told them that I found the cards in the bar and asked if it was the pack they played with last night. When they said it was I showed them the marked petals on the back.'

'Christ!' said Catchpole. '*Christ!*'

He turned his back on me and I wondered whether he was crying.

'I'm afraid your friends can now be counted on the fingers of one mitten.'

The cellar wasn't very bright and he was too far away for me to see his expression, but he was shaking his head again. It seemed to be his standard response to the world this weekend.

'It's a bit of a surprise to find somebody who can treat human beings like this,' he said. It was a strange remark, coming from him.

'Oh, I crossed you off my list of human beings a long time ago,' I told him. He would be free within hours and I was reluctant to pass up this last opportunity for unpleasantness. 'For a thousand pounds I could have you killed. Did you know that?'

'That's what it used to cost. It's a lot more now.'

'No, it isn't,' I told him. 'Rising unemployment has made the chaps with shooters keep their prices competitive.'

I said this with such conviction that he stood up, believing perhaps that I had business contacts with shadowy men in London's East End who removed people from this world, via the River Thames, at very reasonable rates.

'You're off your bloody trolley,' he said.

I paused at that. The situation was, after all, insane. But the only way out now was for me to get him as drunk tonight as he had been last night, and then tell his friends later that I had found him in a stupor in the cellar where he had obviously been taking advantage of my whisky supply. Adam and I would soon transfer him to room seven, and nobody was going to believe his incredible version of what had happened. If they did, nobody was going to be able to prove it.

'Those whom the gods wish to destroy, they first render imbecilic,' I said with a smile. 'Look, I've brought you food.'

I produced the supply of cheese sandwiches from the bag and put them on the floor beside the cell. He looked astonishingly grateful at that, as if, in other circumstances, I had offered to buy him dinner. My motives were less altruistic than he imagined. If he drank the whisky that I was planning for him on an empty stomach he would probably be sick and never achieve the unconsciousness that was fundamental to my programme.

He ate the sandwiches at a frightening speed. I have never seen food vanish so quickly. They seemed to perk him up.

'Great hotel you have here,' he said, staring across at the cold breeze-block wall.

'Luxurious, isn't it?' I said. 'Just remember that there are a million people living in cardboard boxes in Bombay.'

'At least they can go out when they want to.'

'We have the English Tourist Board's seal of approval,' I told him.

The sandwiches had gone.

'What about something to wash them down with?' he asked.

'In a minute. Did you read the press cuttings?'

'Some of them.'

'Pretty interesting stuff, eh? Did you try the finger trick against the wall?'

'Matter of fact, I did. I don't know what all the fuss was about.'

'Of course, it loses much of its charm if there isn't somebody there to smash you across the back at the same time with a rifle.'

He started to pace up and down his cell now, feeling better after eating.

'What's your plan?' he asked.

I was about to tell him, and then realized that it wouldn't work if I did. He would feign drunkenness and then raise hell when the door was unlocked.

'I'm going to hang you from a gibbet,' I said.

'Don't start that again,' he said, almost pleadingly. 'Suppose I make so much noise that people round here start to ask questions?'

'Go ahead. You're much too far away for anyone to hear.'

In fact this wasn't true, but as he had arrived in the cellar unconscious he had no idea where he was. If he had started to shout I could block the noise in the bar with music. A small grille at the top of one wall was at ground level in the yard at the back of the hotel but I was the only person who used that area, mostly to stack empty beer barrels and silver tanks of draught lemonade for collection by the brewery.

'Among your manifold shortcomings,' I said, 'is that you are thick. If you could call help as easily as that I would never have locked you in here.'

Evidently he found this story convincing. 'And when are you going to let me out of here?'

'I've melted the key.'

He came over to the bars and held them up with both hands, the gorilla in the zoo. 'What's your plan?' he said again. 'How does all this end?'

I shrugged. 'It's difficult, isn't it? I don't suppose there is anybody out there daft enough to pay hostage money on you, is there?'

He shook his head. 'A few people would probably pay you money to keep me here.'

'That's what I thought.'

'But somebody will come looking for me eventually and they'll throw the book at you.'

'Which book?' I said. 'I hope it's one by Gordon Williams. I enjoy his novels.'

'The law,' said Catchpole. The mention of the word provided me with a nasty brush with reality.

'I came down to let you out this morning, but you were obviously going to break my neck as soon as I unlocked the door,' I said, swiftly rehearsing my defence. 'You're so violent, Edwin.'

He thought about this for some time and I believe that he saw my problem.

'If I promised . . .' he began, but realized that it was hopeless. 'So here I am.'

'So here you are. The arm of justice is longer than the legs of the traitor, comrade. You'd look just right with electrodes on your head, eating with a rubber spoon.'

For the only time he looked as if he might cry.

'What a great bloody weekend.'

'Into every life some rain must fall.'

'I can hear it,' said Catchpole. It was still pelting outside.
'Do you want anything else to eat?'

'Dry roasted peanuts,' he said. He could see a carton of
them on the floor. I opened it and pushed half a dozen
packets through the bars.

'What about some falling-down lotion?'

'What's that?' I asked.

'Whisky.'

'Certainly,' I said. 'A customer's wish is our command.' I
was greatly relieved that he had asked for the whisky himself. If I had forced it on him he could have become suspicious. 'What brand would you like?'

He scanned the boxes against the wall and entered into the
charade. He had to win my friendship somehow.

'I think I'll have a little J. and B.,' he said. 'Normally I
can't afford it.'

'Justerini and Brooks coming up,' I said. 'A very fine
choice, sir.' I tore open the carton and took a bottle across
to him. I pushed it through the bars and he took the other
end — it was the only contact we had. For a moment he held
it like a weapon and I thought, ridiculously, of the Vietcong,
turning American beer cans into grenades.

'I hope there isn't going to be any violence,' I said. 'I hate
the sight of blood — particularly mine.'

It took him a minute to weigh his need for the Scotch
against the remote possibility of hurting me through the
bars, but I was now standing well back. He began to hug the
bottle in the manner of a man who doesn't like to share.

I stood watching him and wondering how I was going to
cope with the situation tomorrow when he came into the bar
and I had to pretend that this had never happened. 'Good
morning, Mr Catchpole. Are you having a pleasant weekend?' Was duplicity on that scale beyond my reach? And
how would he react? Would he vault the counter and tear my
throat out? Or would he be too embarrassed to meet the

128

friends he had been cheating and slink off home alone?

Of course I had a good hold over him now — my silence about the cards for his good behaviour — but it wasn't one that I wanted to use. The very least that I could do towards the permanent discomfiture of Edwin Catchpole was tell his friends about the marked deck.

'Cheers, cheat,' I said.

'Are you going?' he asked stupidly. Our chats were all he had at the moment.

'Talking to you won't bring in the bread and butter, will it?' I said. 'If you get bored read your press cuttings again.'

I headed for the steps and then remembered that I had not given him enough whisky.

'If you stand back you can have another bottle,' I said. 'It's a long night.'

He retreated immediately to the corner of the cell and I pulled out another bottle of Justerini and Brooks and slid it through the bottom of the bars.

Then I climbed out of the cellar, confident that the problem of the rebarbative resident would soon be over.

10

There were not many people in for dinner that evening. Laurel and I ate at a table by the window so that I could see what business was arriving in the car park at the front.

'What does the *maître d'hôtel* recommend?' she asked, studying the menu.

'The Ritz in Piccadilly is excellent,' I told her, 'and there's a hell of a good spot in Greek Street.'

She had changed now into a white silk shirt and navy jeans. She looked good enough to eat herself.

'And what about the Bali's food?' she asked. 'Livestock in the side salad, and slugs on the hoof?'

'It's more your lumpfish roe than beluga caviar,' I agreed. 'We're still waiting for a rosette for cuisine.'

'I seem to remember that the nosh here is rather good,' said Laurel. 'Did Scott make the steak and kidney pie or was it delivered here frozen?'

'He made it.'

'I'll have it.'

I beckoned Judy and ordered a steak salad with plenty of lettuce for myself. Judy and Laurel talked for a while: they had become very friendly on Laurel's first visit.

'It's a pity I haven't brought the weather with me,' she said when our food arrived. 'Am I talking about the weather? God, I'm boring. The best thing about being me is that you don't have to meet me.'

'You're the most unboring person I know,' I said. 'We'll just have to stay indoors and get drunk.'

'But this place is so beautiful in the sun. I wanted to get out and enjoy the fresh air.'

'Perhaps it will clear up tomorrow.'

'Not according to the little man on television. He was transferring all the rain clouds in his collection to just here.'

'I would sooner live here in the rain than in London in the sun,' I said. 'After a day in London you have to pick your nose for half an hour.' It was in my interests that Laurel preferred here to London, even if the snow was knee deep and the heating out of order.

'I'm no fan of London,' she said obligingly. 'It just happens to be where the money is.'

Judy brought us some red wine and I filled our glasses.

'We're not so cash conscious in the country,' I said. 'Down here life is one long Saturday night.'

'I always understood that some of you country folk were pretty good at accumulating money.'

'Oh, we are,' I said. 'And we're a thousand times better at hanging on to it than your flash city types.'

'I never was deceived by your grubby Peugeot. I've got you down on my list as an incipient millionaire.'

I drank some wine and examined this remark.

'What list would that be?' I asked.

'My short list.'

'Many of us on it?'

'Not many,' she said. 'In fact you're the only one at the moment.'

'That's a relief — I hate competition.'

'I'm glad you're glad.'

Her simple statement hung in the air, demanding a response.

'Look,' I said, 'it's pretty lonely out here on the cusp of Pisces. Why don't you move in?'

Was I proposing matrimony? Hold me back, someone.

'Move in and pretend we're married, do you mean?'

'Absolutely. The price of respectability is eternal hypocrisy, and round here you are respectable or you are nothing.'

'Alternatively, we could actually get married,' said Laurel, putting down her knife and fork and looking at me.

'I accept your proposal,' I said quickly. 'I rather thought marriage wasn't your thing.'

'Marriage is every girl's thing, Martin. You should know that. We're engaged then. That's settled. What's for pudding?'

I wanted to kiss her but it didn't seem the right behaviour for the dining-room of my own hotel. Instead, my fiancée ordered a rupture rapture — whimsically described on my somewhat unorthodox menus as a 'colourful landslide of six flavours of ice-cream, whipped cream, strawberry, peaches, nuts, wafers and chocolate flakes'.

I ordered champagne. Judy raised her eyebrows at this request and hurried off, guessing frantically at its significance.

'Mrs Stapleton will be pleased,' I said.

'How is the old dear?' Laurel asked.

'She's in great form. However, we have a spot of trouble over Adam.'

I told her of the two new guests in room ten.

'I remember Rodney,' she said. 'A terrible little Herbert.'

'It should be fun if he shows up here tonight.'

But when we swept out of the restaurant to announce our engagement to an impatient world there was only Alice Chetwynd Stapleton at the bar, discussing the perversity of the British climate with Moaner Lisa. I poured her a glass of champagne.

'Something has occurred?' she suggested. 'Hallo, Laurel. You look very fetching.'

'We're getting married,' Laurel told her.

'Married?' said Mrs Stapleton. 'Who to?'

'To each other,' I said. She looked as if someone had hit her round the back of the head with a cricket bat.

'Martin and Laurel are getting married,' explained Lisa, who seemed to have less difficulty in absorbing the news.

'Good God,' said Mrs Stapleton, and she jumped from her stool to kiss Laurel on both cheeks. She emerged from this

132

embrace with her wig — pageboy cut tonight — askew.

'Congratulations, Martin. You're brighter than I thought.'

'I knew you'd approve,' I said, pouring Lisa some champagne.

'I'm afraid Adam won't though.'

'He's probably engaged to be married himself by now. He's upstairs with Julie.'

'There must be something in your beer. It's making everyone romantic.'

'Shall we always drink champagne?' Laurel asked. 'I prefer it to wine.'

'Start the way you mean to go on,' said Mrs Stapleton. 'Nail him down now.'

I didn't really believe that Laurel was going to become my wife. It had happened too quickly. But I was enjoying pretending to believe it.

'You can have whatever you want,' I said. 'Just come and get it.'

Mrs Stapleton handed me her empty glass. 'I'll have some more champagne, if you don't mind. An engagement at the Bali is not an everyday event.' I filled her glass and as she and Lisa drank the health of the happy couple I kissed my fiancée for the first time.

'Perhaps I should go on a course,' she said, when I finally released her. 'To learn about hotel management?'

'Are you going to work as well?' I asked. 'I imagined that you would just fill the place with your loveliness.'

'That would be very wise of you, dear,' said Mrs Stapleton. 'A wife can't know too much.'

'I've never been much in favour of work,' I admitted.

'Carlyle might have believed that all work was noble. Martin does not,' said Mrs Stapleton.

Laurel turned to Lisa. 'Does he work hard?'

'Very,' said Lisa. All my staff thought I worked too hard, mainly because I was on duty seven days a week.

'Don't tell them,' I said. 'It spoils my playboy image.'

At that moment the fruit machine king came in, his chart protruding from the pocket of his wet jacket, and immediately behind him was Rodney.

'Excuse me,' I said to Laurel. 'I have an urgent message for room ten.'

There was a long silence when I knocked on the bedroom door, but Adam's muffled voice eventually called to ask who it was. When I told him, the door was opened by Julie, who was totally naked. Her tall slim body was revealed to be surprisingly shapely.

'Come in,' she said. I stepped inside and shut the door. Adam was in bed, looking slightly worn. Julie just stood there, making no pretence of reaching for clothes. I decided later that she was so dazed by the excitements of the last hour that she had forgotten that she had no clothes on.

'Rodney's just come in,' I told them. 'I thought I should let you know.'

'What did he say?' Julie asked.

'He said he'd die for you.'

'He said that?'

'Swing for you, was the phrase he used. No, I'm only joking. I haven't spoken to him yet.'

'Don't tell him we're here,' Adam said.

'Your car's outside,' I pointed out.

'I often leave it in your car park. I thought you'd have noticed by now.'

'By the way,' I said, 'I just became engaged.'

'To Laurel?'

I nodded.

'Funny thing. I just became engaged as well,' said Adam. Julie giggled.

'Congratulations. Come down for a celebration drink later,' I suggested.

'We sure will. Come here, Jool. I've just thought of a new game.'

I hurried out before his latest sexual frolic could get under way. When I got downstairs I was encouraged to see that Lisa was giving Laurel lessons in how to pull a pint. At the counter, Rodney Pym, his fist wrapped round a whisky, was telling Mrs Stapleton, 'Adam is going to find himself in hospital on a life-support system.'

134

'Oh, stop it, Rodney,' she said. 'I'm a coward and you don't even frighten me.'

He flushed angrily, 'I'll fix him. You'll see.'

'Good evening, Rodney,' I said. 'Thanks for the lunch.'

I was trying to be polite — I had forgotten that in the end he had refused to pay for it.

'Very funny,' he snarled. 'If you think I'm going to buy that bastard lunch, you're crazy. Who did pay, by the way?'

'Chad. He said you'd settle with him later.'

Rodney's lips tightened at this news. I imagined that he didn't want to alienate Chad. Between that and paying for Adam's lunch he had a difficult course to steer. I wasn't about to help him.

'Where did they go?' he asked.

'They?'

'Julie and Adam.'

'I've no idea,' I said. I have no compunction about lying professionally, especially when my hotel will be wrecked if I don't. 'They can't have gone for a walk in this rain.'

'He's not at home.'

I was glad that he hadn't noticed Adam's van outside. With this weather it could only mean that he was here. But later when I sauntered over to the window I saw that Adam had had the sense to park at the back, where we had once unloaded crates of bitter lemon in the middle of the night.

'What do you think of it, anyway?' Rodney demanded, sitting glumly on his stool.

'Think of what?' asked Mrs Stapleton.

'A chap stealing your wife.'

It is one of several disadvantages to my job that I am not able to discuss certain matters with uninhibited candour. I have to observe the amenities. Fortunately, Mrs Stapleton is under no such restraint.

'Come off it, Rodney,' she said, laughing. 'Nobody ever steals anybody's wife. Men lose their own wives is what happens.'

'Quite,' said Laurel, obviously about to enjoy an analysis of the institution she had recently decided to join. 'By cruelty or

135

neglect or meanness or adultery. Which was it in your case?'

Rodney looked at her as if he would knock her off the stool.

'This is my fiancée,' I said quickly. 'You met her a few weeks ago when she was here.'

'You getting married, Martin?' he asked, peering at me over his spectacles. 'Best of bloody luck.'

'Adam hardly enticed her away from you with his money, did he?' said Mrs Stapleton, laughing again. 'So it must be something else. Did you hit her?'

Rodney blushed and said nothing.

'Adam hasn't your talent for making money, Rodney, but he is a gentle man, a kind man, a man who would make a girl feel appreciated and wanted and loved. Money isn't very important if a relationship between a man and a woman is right, and it's certainly no substitute for the things I just mentioned.'

Mrs Stapleton sat back proudly after delivering this short speech and drank deeply from her champagne glass. I opened a fresh bottle with a decidedly plebeian pop and filled everybody's glass.

'We'd only been married a year,' Rodney said. 'We'd hardly got going.'

'Well, she's got going,' said Mrs Stapleton. 'In fact she's gone.'

'It seems to give you some pleasure, Alice,' said Rodney, with a harsh tone to his voice.

'I want the woman to be happy,' said Mrs Stapleton chirpily. 'I am in favour of women being happy.'

'She's good, isn't she?' Laurel said to me. 'I hope you've taken in what she's been saying.'

'Martin's all right, dear,' Mrs Stapleton told her. 'A few misguided ideas about down-trodden males, but basically sound.'

'Give me another Scotch,' said Rodney. 'Let's see if I can get breathalysed two nights running.'

An hour later, when Rodney had drunk three more, Adam appeared alone at the door of the room. He didn't look like Adam at all. He looked younger and more awake and his hair had been combed differently with a new parting. Julie had obviously put her stamp on him already.

He came over to the bar and I braced myself for the sound of porridge hitting a fan.

'Good evening, everybody, and hallo, Laurel,' he said. He took her hand and kissed it. 'I've been hearing some stories about you and there are one or two facts I want to bring to your notice before you become part-owner of this establishment. Fact one: Adam can always get a drink here, regardless of the licensing hours. Fact two: Adam can always drink on credit when he's short of the readies.'

'Fact three: Adam is always available to do you a favour,' I said, thinking of the midnight mission I had lined up for him in the cellar. I poured him some champagne. Rodney was now staring into his whisky as if he was too embarrassed to acknowledge that Adam had arrived.

Adam ignored him and lifted his glass to us. 'Prosit!'

Rodney pulled himself round on the stool at the sound of his voice and said, 'There you are, Adam.' Perhaps he was drunk and had genuinely not seen him come in. 'Where's my wife?'

'I believe she's having a shower.'

'I asked where she was.'

'Ah,' said Adam. 'The bathroom. That's where ·they put the shower.'

'Which bloody bathroom?'

'Look,' I said, 'if you gentlemen want to talk can you do it somewhere else?'

'I certainly want to talk to Adam,' said Rodney, very solemnly.

'Anywhere, pal.'

'Let's adjourn to a corner, then.'

He got off his stool and took Adam's elbow. Together they walked to the farthest corner of the room.

'Will they fight?' asked Mrs Stapleton. 'Is somebody going to get a mouthful of knuckles?'

'Not in here,' I said, watching them.

'Oh, what a shame.'

'Is it as exciting as this in here every night?' asked Laurel. 'I don't think I could stand it.'

The two men sat down on opposite sides of a window table, Rodney hunched forward with his arms resting on the table and his hands meeting round the whisky glass, and Adam sitting back, his seat balanced on the rear two legs and his arms casually folded. Rodney was doing the talking. I was watching them carefully because of the possibility of my table being hoisted aloft by one man and broken over the skull of the other, to the detriment of my table, but the talking went on and on, with no raised voices or hints of violence.

I had to stop watching when the bar began to fill up. Among the new customers were Gordon Hammerdale and his party. They had been eating in the restaurant.

'Any news?' he asked.

'News?'

'Catchpole.'

'Oh, no. Have you?'

'Not a sign of him.'

'Let me know if he shows up,' I said.

I fetched the pints with which they customarily launched the evening's drinking. One of them had noticed Laurel.

'I wonder who she has breakfast with?' he said.

'Me,' I told him.

'There you are, Keith, getting into trouble again,' said Gordon Hammerdale. 'He never thinks before he speaks. He just opens his mouth and lets the wind blow his tongue about.'

From across the room came the chunk-chunk-chunk of another fruit machine jackpot. I rejoined the ladies.

'I haven't felt like this since last night,' said Mrs Stapleton, reaching for her champagne. 'I've been telling Laurel what a good thing husbands are.'

'Did you tell her what happened to yours?'

'Yes, and she told me what happened to her brother Timothy.'

'That's two strange deaths I've heard about this weekend,' I said, remembering.

'They happen in threes,' said Mrs Stapleton. 'So watch it.'

'When I was small Timothy used to tie me to a tree and throw darts at me,' said Laurel.

Mrs Stapleton nodded, as if it was no more than she would expect. 'Aren't children lovely?' she said.

'Did you ever have any?' Laurel asked.

'No, I did not,' she replied firmly. 'I thought it would be an act of great selfishness. Who are all these parents satisfying except themselves?'

'I bet there's more to it than that,' Laurel said.

'Well, to be frank, I don't understand the magic appeal of kids. They're only people waiting to become boring adults. In fact, I sometimes think of taking up child-throttling. I think it could become a cult.'

Adam suddenly appeared on the stool beside her. I looked round. There was no sign of Rodney.

'I don't believe it,' Adam said.

'Neither do I,' said Mrs Stapleton, 'but I pretend that I do.'

'What happened?'

'He offered me five thousand pounds if I promised not to see Julie again.'

'Where are we going?' asked Mrs Stapleton. 'I hear Nassau is pleasant at this time of year.'

'Jesus,' said Adam.

'Is that what he values her at?' Laurel said.

'No, it's what he values Adam's price at,' I said. 'What did you tell him?'

'I told him to stuff it up his trousers, or words to that effect.'

'Was that wise?' Mrs Stapleton asked. 'It could be the capital you need.'

'Good God, Alice, I love her,' Adam said. 'Don't you understand?'

'No, I don't,' said Mrs Stapleton. 'It was only yesterday that you were telling me how unnecessary women were.'

'Yesterday I didn't know that the woman I love is in love with me.'

'Well, I'm very happy for you. On the other hand, five thousand smackers is five thousand smackers. Couldn't you take the loot and pick her up later?'

Adam ignored Mrs Stapleton's suggestion, which struck me as being basically sound, and looked dazed but happy.

'She has that look in her eyes which persuades a man that he should reproduce himself,' he said. 'It's certainly persuaded me.'

'Oh, not all that breeding stuff again,' said Mrs Stapleton. 'Life is a sexually transmitted disease.'

'You're a cynical old bat, Mrs Stapleton,' said Adam. 'Try some more champagne.'

Suddenly Mrs Stapleton looked sad. 'I am old,' she said. 'And I am cynical. The only hope I have left is to die painlessly.'

A wave of depression engulfed me when she said that: for me she always epitomized fun. The mood was broken by Lisa, who said that Adam was wanted on the internal phone. He returned smiling.

'I've been summoned to room ten,' he said. 'Julie won't come down in case Rodney returns.'

'When duty calls,' said Mrs Stapleton. 'It killed Attila the Hun, you know.'

'What did?'

'Sex.'

'The painless death you were talking about,' said Adam, finishing his champagne.

When he had gone I refilled our glasses and struggled to remember that I was now engaged to be married myself.

Going to bed with women was once a routinely straightforward matter, like washing your socks. It became difficult suddenly when books and magazines began to carry long and solemn essays raising simple pleasure to esoteric art. Veteran lovers discovered to their horror that their performances were hopelessly flawed. Besieged by a doubt which they had never expected and could barely comprehend, they began to wonder whether sexual intercouse was best left to the experts. Instead of making love they stood around sheepishly and talked about it. What did 'coital orgasmic inadequacy' mean? Was heterosexual intercourse on the way out? Was it only women who

140

knew what a woman wanted? Was tribadism the coming thing? Was sex political?

Abortive searches were launched for undiscovered erogenous zones.

In the country the sound like a drone of bees was more likely to be the new sexual vibrators than a drone of bees, and respectable magazines which had once fed women on a mild diet of jam recipes and knitting patterns now shrieked wantonly: IS YOUR PARTNER SENSITIVE TO THE STIMULATION YOU WANT?

When a man met a pretty girl for the first time he no longer imagined her with no clothes on: he wondered morosely what she had been reading. Fatigue, impotence and inhibition became the standard response to the certainty of sex.

The birth-rate dropped for the first time in fifty years.

Men whose energy had previously been discharged between the silk sheets of a double bed sought other outlets for their strength. Millions of middle-aged men across three continents took up jogging.

The detumescent effect of the sexual revolution passed me by because I ignored it: the sight of an earnest researcher sends me into a comatose heap, and I regard distrust of the self-appointed expert as fundamental to a balanced personality.

One of Laurel's many virtues was that the sexual revolution missed her, too. Her attitude to sex was the wisest one — that it was not only fun but funny.

'Get your knickers off,' was her opening shot in the bedroom.

Clothes were never shed so quickly.

'Wow,' said Laurel.

'Open your legs and say ouch,' I told her.

It is impossible to remember all the things we did that night but my large bed, peculiarly cosy with the rain beating against the windows, was a busy place to be. Lettuce emerged from the imbroglio (or should I say seraglio?) with its reputation considerably enhanced, but the credit went to me.

'One more time,' said Laurel. This was two hours into the

main event and she had taken to lying on her back and not doing very much.

'Are you keeping the score?' I asked.

'Monographs from this source will follow shortly.'

'Just six more times, then?'

'Don't tell me — you were in the Swiss navy as well.'

She had a body that invited assault. Its shape seemed to remain the same no matter which way she was lying. Occasionally she slid into unexpected action herself. 'One swallow doesn't make a blow job,' she gurgled at one stage.

In the respites that grew longer as the night wore on, Laurel talked of our marriage. She wanted it to take place here, in the country, and not in London.

'We can swan off on honeymoon and leave the guests paying to stay in the hotel,' she said. 'Clever, eh? We'll be rich beyond the dreams of the average.'

'No honeymoon in Pamplona though,' I said.

'Monaco,' said Laurel. 'I decided that my honeymoon would be in Monaco years ago. Can't you see me topless among the toffs?'

I found this picture so provocative that it was a quarter of an hour before we talked again.

'I hope you're not like this every night,' said Laurel. 'I could look old before my time.'

Once I fell asleep but woke up quickly remembering something. Then Laurel dozed and I woke her by drawing on her back.

'I have to go downstairs,' I said. 'I won't be long.'

'In the middle of the night?' she murmured sleepily. 'You're not going anywhere.' She turned on her side and held me in a hug.

I lay there struggling for a sensible excuse; the truth was beyond explaining. I couldn't see the time on my watch, but working on from when I had last known it I guessed that it was soon after four. I had to get down to the cellar, unlock the door, and then come back up again to extract Adam from his *Lovefest*. My story for him was simple: I had heard noises in the cellar and when I went down to investigate had discovered the missing Catchpole surrounded by empty whisky bottles.

All I needed now was a story to tell Laurel, who had fallen asleep again hugging me.

I eased myself free but it woke her.

'Stay!' she said firmly, as if to a dog.

My mind groped for one valid, convincing reason to go downstairs at four o'clock in the morning, but the ones that I thought up — the sound of breaking glass, a burglar, bottles being broken or shifted — were too dramatic and would have Laurel insisting on coming with me.

I lay in the dark, fighting to concentrate. In the end I gently eased myself free from Laurel's embrace and then lay motionless, waiting for her breathing to tell me that she was deeply asleep. If I didn't risk disturbing her by looking for my clothes, which had coins and keys ready to jangle in the pockets, I could slip silently from the room.

But champagne and sex undermine that willpower which keeps you awake when your body wants to sleep, and suddenly I had drifted off into a very deep sleep that held me for five hours until the darkness and the incessant rain had been replaced by a bright morning sunshine. And bliss was it that dawn to be asleep because once I had woken it was all horror.

Part Four

Monday

11

It was the time of year when the birds belied their bird-brain reputation and showed a brighter intelligence than the two-legged mammals who lumbered below. Swallows flocked on overhead wires and housemartins gathered on rooftops to plan epic journeys to the south. If they could avoid the guns in Spain, they would follow the sun all the way to Africa.

On the other side of the river the leaves on the silver birch trees were turning yellow, and the sandy slopes that encouraged the pine trees and the heather were covered in flawless pine cones that people collected and saved for Christmas decoration.

It was the inhospitable sand which sent eighteen hours of rain down to the river, producing a volume which the banks could not contain. It was a gentle irruption compared with some of the great floods of the past but it was still sufficient to invade my land because once the footpath at the side of the river was breached the water discovered a leisurely downhill journey to the Bali's grounds.

My marrow patch was the first to go, and then the vegetable garden, which I had begun as an economy and continued as a labour of love. Cabbages, beetroot, carrots and some potatoes that I was planning to lift vanished beneath the invasion. The lawn, which separated the garden from the patio, came next. It trickled across my newly mown grass, not even reaching the bottom of the children's swing seats, which were especially low for toddlers. Progress would have been easier when it reached the stone floor of the patio, washing the legs of my white plastic furniture and carrying twigs and leaves and mud round to the yard where Adam had hidden his van and empty beer kegs awaited the draymen's collection.

But the flood's inexorable progress was still not spent because some time that night, when it washed up against the walls of the hotel itself, it discovered a natural escape in the air vents at the top of the cellar's wall.

I woke in a panic, knowing something was seriously wrong. It came to me at once — I had not released Catchpole.

I jumped from the bed with a force that wakened Laurel and went, as usual, to the window. I stared aghast at the flooded garden. If an Irish warrior priest had been arriving in a coracle I wouldn't have been more surprised.

'Christ!' I said, hurling my clothes on.

'What is it?'

'Floods,' I told her.

She got out of bed herself to have a look but I was already leaving the room.

I had time to think going downstairs, and I realized that whatever had happened a display of panic by me would be hopelessly incriminating. By the time I reached the ground floor I was my usual placid self.

The breakfast-eaters had already left the restaurant and I went through to the kitchen to see Scott.

'The sun has come out for us motor-cyclists,' he said.

'Won't it be too wet?'

'We love it wet. Have you seen the floods?'

'Yes, how bad are they?'

'They're nothing compared with the last one, but I expect the cellar's a bit wet. I went to check but you seem to have locked it.'

'Did I lock it? I must have been drunk. I'll go and check it myself.'

I steeled myself to walk calmly down the cellar steps, afraid of what I might find. The water that had poured through the air vent was not deep but it covered the floor. I waded through it, not thinking of my shoes and socks, and unlocked the cell. Catchpole lay in the far corner.

To reduce the number of people who were buried alive, they used to fasten bells to the toes of corpses and leave them for forty-eight hours. This would not be necessary in the case of Edwin Catchpole.

Lying on his back he would have emerged with little worse than a soaked suit. But he was lying face down on the floor and he had drowned in three inches of water. I turned him over to make sure that he was dead. His face was bluish and several small spots had appeared on his cheeks.

'Who the hell is that?' Laurel's voice asked.

I turned to see that she had followed me into the cellar and was standing now on the bottom step, an inch or two above the water level.

'It's a customer,' I said coolly.

'Is he all right?'

'He's exhibiting what the CIA call a hundred-per-cent mortality response,' I said.

A guilty man wouldn't reply so lightly.

'Why was he locked in?'

'Locked in?'

'Yes, locked in.'

'He wasn't locked in.' I tried to remember my story. 'He obviously came down here to pinch some whisky, got drunk and fell asleep.'

'There's a key in the door. You had him locked in there, didn't you?' Her voice had risen since her arrival. 'What the hell are you playing at, Martin?'

I abandoned Catchpole and waded back to my accuser.

'He is a resident who has been missing since yesterday morning. Perhaps he's been here since then. Perhaps he's had a heart attack.'

'He was locked in,' she repeated. She had got hold of the one relevant fact in a confusing situation and seemed reluctant to let it go. Her tone was now a chilling mixture of fear and anger.

I put a hand on her shoulder.

'Let's make sure we're singing out of the same hymn book,' I said. 'He was drunk. There are two whisky bottles by his body.'

She turned her back on me and climbed the steps.

'We'd better call the police,' she said.

'Of course we must,' I replied, and followed her.

We went into my office, my feet dripping, and I dialled the police station. Laurel sat on the edge of my desk and watched.

I decided to persist with my performance of guiltless observer. I cupped my hand over the receiver and told her, 'I've now got three months' supply of wet roasted peanuts.'

She gave me a long, strange look, and I knew that whatever else was going to come out of this, our romance was over.

A day that had started so badly was beyond saving. By lunchtime a dose of bilharziasis would have been a welcome distraction.

A detective constable arrived first in a black Ford Granada. He assured me, as if I cared, that the police surgeon was on his way. The detective took off his boots and socks, rolled up his trousers and waded round the cellar taking photographs.

I expressed surprise and concealed alarm.

'We always take pictures of the body if there is a faint possibility of foul play, Mr Lomax,' he said.

'Foul play?'

'Where death in unusual situations occurs the police always have to consider foul play. Have you moved the body?'

'I turned him over to see if he was dead.'

'A pity.'

His eyes roved round the cellar and settled on the lock on the cell door. I felt a wave of fear then. Tenacity was not the quality I was seeking in this man.

'He was drunk,' I said. 'He had obviously been stealing my whisky.'

'How do you know he was drunk?'

I began to see how people can talk themselves into trouble: there was really no reason for me to say anthing at all.

'It's just an educated guess,' I said. 'There are two empty whisky bottles alongside the body.'

The police surgeon arrived soon afterwards. He was a small, grey-haired man who was surprisingly cheerful, given

150

his macabre calling. In the midst of life he was in death.

'Epileptics and drunks die this way,' he said, when I ventured to point out how shallow the water was. 'Epileptics have been known to have a fit, fall into a puddle and drown.'

He threw me a smile which seemed to say that it would be a long time before I heard anything half so whimsical, but nobbled by a mixture of fatigue and nausea I could only stare back.

'Has the cellar flooded before?' the detective asked.

'Several times,' I said. 'But there wasn't anybody in it then.'

'Why is there a lock on the door?'

'My father used to lock his precious wines away.'

'Where's the key?'

'I don't know,' I said, feeling it in my pocket. 'I have a more trusting attitude to my staff.'

'And you think —' he looked at his notebook ' — Mr Catchpole came down here for some quiet drinking and got drunk?'

'It looks like that to me.'

'The *post mortem* will soon tell us,' said the police surgeon. 'There are no gunshot wounds or blows to the head.'

'Any daggers in the back?' I asked.

'I'm afraid not. It's very disappointing.'

'I imagine the whisky could have killed him before the cellar flooded,' I suggested.

'It could, but I don't think it did,' said the police surgeon. 'The most likely cause of death here is asphyxia, because he was not able to draw in air through the mouth or nose. Can you phone for a wagon, George? We'll take him in for the PM.'

He stared down at the late Mr Catchpole, while the detective sat on the steps trying to dry his feet.

'What happens at a *post mortem*?' I asked. I had often wondered — you never know where you are going to end up.

'We cut him up,' said the police surgeon with a sort of relish. 'We inspect all the organs, record all the findings. In this case the main objective will be to determine the blood-alcohol level.'

'Actually the pathologist cuts him up,' said the detective, pulling up his socks.

'Ah, but I'm there,' said the police surgeon.

My mind moved on to the next immediate problem. Carrying a corpse out of the front door of a hotel was traditionally regarded as bad for business, alarming residents, discouraging visitors and reflecting adversely on the establishment's cuisine.

'Can you ask the wagon to pull up at the back?' I asked.

'Certainly,' said the detective, tying up his boots. 'Can you show me to a phone?'

We went up to my office. The hotel was empty. It was too early for the bar to be open and the first sun in four days had evidently dispersed the guests.

The detective phoned the police station and then sat down with his notebook. A much chewed pencil appeared from his pocket.

'Now what about next-of-kin?' he asked. 'Have you got this joker's address?'

'It's in the visitors' book,' I said. 'He was here with some friends from Yorkshire, playing golf.'

'It wasn't his weekend, was it?' said the police surgeon.

I picked up the house phone and rang through to Gordon Hammerdale's room.

'Hallo?' he said. I had woken him up.

'Mr Hammerdale? We've found your friend Catchpole. Can you come down to reception?'

'Where did he get to?'

'He's dead.'

There was a long silence on the phone and I hung up.

'One of his mates is coming down,' I told the policeman.

'I've known a bottle of whisky kill a man,' said the police surgeon, while we waited. 'How many singles are there in a bottle?'

'Thirty,' I told him.

'Eighteen gives you a blood-alcohol count of about three

152

hundred milligrams to a hundred millilitres of blood. That puts you in danger of death.'

I don't know where you police get your figures from,' I said. 'I have several customers who drink ten double whiskies and drive home apparently sober.'

'I must tell our traffic patrol,' said the detective constable. Gordon Hammerdale arrived soon afterwards, pale and unshaven.

'Did you say dead?' he asked.

'I'm afraid so.'

'Are you a member of Mr Catchpole's party?' asked the detective.

Hammerdale nodded. He looked as if words were beyond his powers at the moment. The detective told him what had happened. Hammerdale listened carefully and when he finally spoke it took no little control to restrain myself from throwing my arms round him and kissing both cheeks.

'He's done it before,' he said.

'What?' said the detective.

'He was found drunk once in the cellar of a pub at home.'

'What happened? Be precise.'

'He was drunk at closing time one night and they wouldn't serve any more drinks. He said he was going for a pee and slipped down to the cellar instead. The gaffer found him plastered an hour later when he went down to clean the pipes. He treated it as a joke — Catchpole was one of his best customers.'

I could feel the doubts and suspicions which my nervous pessimism had sensed in the office evaporate.

'That's it, then,' said the detective. The notebook, with its sinister overtones, was restored to his jacket pocket. He stood up. 'It will be necessary for you, as a personal friend, to identify the body.'

Hammerdale nodded sadly. Just then a young policeman arrived at the door.

'I've brought the wagon,' he said.

'Take it round the back,' said the detective.

The four of them filed out of my office but I didn't feel up to following them. Too many unconnected thoughts were clamouring for my foggy attention. Where was Laurel? How did I get the water out of the cellar? Would I soon be appearing in the witness-box at an inquest?

I tried to re-establish some connection with the real world by picking up that morning's copy of *The Times*, which lay on the desk in front of me. I was surprised to discover that it was Bank Holiday Monday — I was losing track of time. There didn't seem to be much news. In Castelgandolfo the Pope had made a controversial call for world peace. There was a funfair on Hampstead Heath, a carnival in Notting Hill and a festival in Edinburgh. It was hot in Ajaccio, but cool in Cape Town.

I put down the paper and another stray thought filtered through: I was supposed to be cooking the lunch.

I specialized in the sort of menu which curbs a man's appetite. When I was substitute chef at the Bali it took a certain resilience to eat there: we who are about to dine salute you.

The eight-ring stove was less important than my Philips micro-wave oven and the vegetable-warmer and plate-warmer alongside. But my main aids were two six-foot fridges and an even larger freezer in the corner of the room.

After five minutes in the kitchen I had decided on my menu and I went back to my office to type three copies: soup of the day (whatever that meant); steak, chips and peas; coq au vin; scampi and chips. Ice cream or apple pie followed. Every one of these items, except the soup, came out of the freezer or the fridge, and I marvelled at how easy Scott's life could be if his professional pride was not offended by the use of frozen chips.

Mrs Newman, housewife, mother of three and aspirant waitress, arrived at twelve and laid the tables. She spent her life on the Bali's substitute bench and was always ready to deputize for someone.

'Tell them it's a limited menu because of the holiday,' I said. 'If they get shirty, smash them over the head with the water jug.'

Mrs Newman, a small, prematurely grey lady, chuckled away quietly. She enjoyed it at the Bali because it got her out of the house.

'Why were the police leaving here as I arrived?' she asked.

'A routine visit, Mrs Newman,' I said.

She went out and returned with an order.

'Two soups, two steaks. They're residents.'

'Has Lisa opened the bar?'

'Yes, but there's only Mrs Stapleton, Adam and Rodney Pym's wife in there.'

I wanted to be with them, feeling particularly in need of a drink, but as I have constantly to remind myself, it's the people who put work first who have money in this world.

'I wonder what he's doing with her — Adam with Rodney Pym's wife?'

'Is he with her?'

'They're holding hands.'

Thank God that's all they're holding, I wanted to tell her. Instead, I said, 'I think you've come across some scandal there, Mrs Newman.'

'That's what I thought. She only married Rodney Pym last year.'

'I should think a year is a long time to be married to Rodney Pym.'

'He's a very ambitious and successful man.'

'Yes, I don't like him either,' I said. 'What was that order again?'

'Soup.'

'In a basket?'

Mrs Newman chuckled her quiet chuckle and I decided that it was time to work. I fetched two soup plates from the pile and tried to concentrate on the job in hand. In Andalucia they may have produced a memorable soup by using the technique of the cocido to marry the broad bean to the cuttle-fish, but round here it was less exotic.

I reached for the can opener.

*　　*　　*

Gordon Hammerdale's dampened golfing party were the last group to come in for lunch. By the time they were on the ice-cream I was able to abandon my chef's role in the kitchen and join them. They were understandably subdued: golfing parties were not normally rained on for two days and then decimated.

'We were just wondering whether we ought to telephone Edwin's father,' Gordon Hammerdale said.

'The police will probably have sent someone round,' I told him, 'but if you want to ring him you can use my phone.'

'Perhaps I should.' He made no move to get up. 'Now the sun has come out none of us feels like golf.'

'What's his father like?'

'He's a bastard. A big bullying bastard.'

'A bit like Edwin,' said a man across the table.

'Edwin was all right,' said Gordon Hammerdale quickly, ready to stifle any posthumous reservations about Catchpole's character. 'But if you ring his dad up and tell him his son's dead, he'll probably say, "Well, bury the bugger." '

This harsh estimate of Catchpole Senior's exiguous seam of human kindness reduced us to a thoughtful silence, and eventually I stood up to leave.

'When are you all going?' I asked.

'We're driving up later this afternoon,' said Gordon Hammerdale. 'I'll settle the bill now.'

He stood up, too, and we went out to my office. The bill came to £236 and he wrote out a cheque.

'I haven't charged for Mr Catchpole,' I pointed out.

'Send the bill to his father,' he said. 'That'll slow the bastard down.'

'Has he left his father any money, do you think?'

'Debts, more like.'

At that moment the telephone rang. I recognized the voice of the detective constable who had spent the morning wading round my cellar.

'Mr Lomax? We've just got the result of the *post mortem*.

156

The alcohol level in Mr Catchpole's blood indicates that he was not conscious when he drowned. I thought you'd like to know. It's the end of the matter really, but there will be an inquest.'

'Will I have to attend?'

'I'm afraid so.'

'Have you been in touch with his father?'

'Funny sod, he is. Our man went round and broke it to him that his son was dead. Know what he said?'

'Tell me.'

'He said, "Well, bury the bugger." '

As soon as I had rid myself of Gordon Hammerdale, I rang through to my room to speak to Laurel, but there was no reply. I rang Adam.

'Have you seen Laurel?' I asked.

'Not today.'

'Listen, Adam. I've got a problem. Can you put your trousers on? They're those things you used to wear below your waist.'

'I'll be down.'

He appeared in my office ten minutes later looking like a man who had barely survived a gruelling physical ordeal.

'Got any milk?' he asked.

I fetched a pint from the kitchen and he drank it without taking the bottle from his lips.

'You have to replace the juices,' he said. 'What's the problem?'

I told him what had happened.

'First thing I've got to do is get the water out of the cellar.' I explained to him how this could be done.

First we found an old tin bath at the back of the hotel, carried it between us down to the cellar and placed it against the wall under the air vents. Floating on the water it began to move away from where we wanted it and we jammed it against the wall with three soggy cartons of Scotch. Then we found a plastic bucket to scoop up the water and fill up the bath. Finally I found a length of rubber tubing that I had used before for the same job. I left Adam in the cellar filling the bath and took the tubing out to the yard. The floods in the garden were disappearing now and the morning's sun had even produced some dry patches on the patio. I fed the tubing through the air vent and down to Adam standing beside the bath, and when he had immersed his end I sucked long and hard on mine as if I was syphoning petrol from a car. Soon the water began to pour out into the yard and I lined up a row of buckets, transferring the tubing as each was filled. The water I returned to the river.

I don't know how many trips I made to the river that afternoon. I counted the first twenty and then lost count. After two hours Adam shouted up that what water was left could be mopped up with old newspapers, and I put the buckets away and went down to see him.

'I think I've just paid for my stay in this joint, pal.'

'There will be no bill,' I promised. 'I'm very impressed that you've still got the energy.'

Lying on the floor I saw the Harrods bag in which I had delivered Catchpole's sandwiches. It gave me a brief fright until I realized that it would have meant nothing to the police. I collected the boxes of formerly dry roasted peanuts and took them upstairs to the dustbins, beside which was a four-foot pile of old newspapers. I took some down to the cellar, where Adam was drying his feet, and laid them on the floor.

'You seem to be having quite a weekend,' Adam said.

'I would have preferred yours.'

'Ugly men stealing your whisky, beautiful women stealing your body.'

I could see that my weekend looked different from where he was.

He put his socks in his pocket and slipped his shoes on. 'I wouldn't be at all amazed if I didn't have a powerful thirst this evening. What time will you open the bar?'

I shrugged. The exertions of the last two hours, following the trauma of this morning — itself coming after a night that was cruelly short of sleep — had filled my head with cotton wool.

'It could be pretty damn early,' I said.

The roar of Scott's Yamaha met us as we came out of the cellar. I was glad to hear it. As he and Judy arrived at the front door in their big white crash helmets they looked like a couple of spacemen.

'How was the motor-cycling?' I asked.

'Magic,' said Scott.

'I think you should take it up,' Judy said. 'You need a sport.'

'I gave up sport as soon as I was old enough to drink,' I said. 'Can you step into my office? I have a proposition for you.' They followed me into the room, gently easing off their crash helmets.

'How would you like next weekend off?' I asked.

'We could go to St Ives,' said Judy. 'You've been promising all summer.'

'What's the catch?' asked Scott.

'Cook dinner tonight. There won't be many in.'

'Too much for you, is it? I thought this was my day off.'

'But next weekend you can have three days off. You can be in St Ives by Friday lunchtime. Listen,' I said, 'I've had a hell of a day.'

I gave them my edited version of what had happened.

'Now is the time for any good party to come to the aid of this man,' I told them.

'Who took the body out?' Judy asked.

'The police.'

'That must have done us a lot of good,' said Scott.

'It was a bit of a social minus,' I agreed. 'Adam and I have spent the afternoon cleaning out the cellar. I'm dirty and I'm knackered, so if you could take over tonight's cooking I would be most grateful.'

I looked at Judy; in my experience if you want to get a decision out of a married couple, you ask the wife.

'Okay,' she said. 'As it's you.'

'Thanks,' I said, as they moved to go. Then Judy turned at the door.

'By the way, has Laurel gone?'

'Gone?'

'We saw her at the station with a suitcase.'

Give me credit — I didn't blink.

It is strange how a woman can fill a room with her tiny presence and, no matter how short her stay, how empty that room can seem when she has gone. The bedroom seemed to be unoccupied and it was hard to believe that this was how it normally looked and had looked only a day ago. The bathroom, of course, was worse, cleared suddenly of her cosmetic armoury.

I looked round for a note — there is always a note — and at first I couldn't find it. I had expected it to be lying prominently on the bed, a dainty grenade device for blowing up hopes, but I found it eventually propped up against the radio. It consisted of three sheets of lined paper torn, apparently, from a notebook in her luggage. She did not travel with envelopes. The pages were covered with neat handwriting in a green felt-nib pen, but it was some time before I read it. I felt that I had endured enough psychological buffeting for one day.

I lay on the bed trying to summon up enough energy to take a shower. Perhaps I slept. After some time I reached across for the note and read it quickly, as if it could hurt. Unlike her last letter, which I had read many times, I only read this one once:

Excuse me while I make a bolt for the train. I am all in favour of a resurgence of the entrepreneurial spirit which once made this country great, but private enterprise prisons are pushing the concept too far. Where will it end? Here in the sticks the days of the mad wife chained in the attic are presumably not over.

Perhaps I will discover the truth about it in the newspapers. By tomorrow you could be a front page story. But I know that you had that man locked up in the cellar and you lied about it and it frightens me to death. It was a

160

mind-boggling lesson in how little we really know of people even when we think we know them. Perhaps you were involved in a joke that misfired, but it didn't look that way to me and nor did your behaviour afterwards.

Anyway, I'm off before the local constable invites me to make a statement. Never talk to strange policemen is a Sherman family motto. This might not be the shortest engagement in human history, but it could get a mention in the record books.

I will resist the temptation to tell you how sad that makes me. I had thought you were different, but hadn't quite realized how different.

Your secret is safe with me. What a pity that I am not safe with you.

Ciao

12

Of all the weaknesses that our comfortable civilization has produced, the reluctance to move has always struck me as the most reprehensible. Man creates his own world in the smallest possible acreage and seems strangely unwilling to escape over the fence. However, it became apparent that evening that this widespread modern infirmity was less than rampant among the users of the Bali Hotel.

Within an hour of opening the bar I had sold it. Mrs Stapleton had called in for her usual cocktails and returned home to eat briefly before the serious drinking, and I was alone at the counter, refreshed equally by a cold shower and a large whisky, when Chad the Impaler walked into the hotel. He walked in like a man who was pricing it.

'I thought I ought to drop in and see your caravanserai,' he said. 'I didn't realize until yesterday that you owned this joint.'

'Hallo, Chad,' I replied. 'Have a drink on the house. *Sur la maison*.' He used to come top in French.

'I'll have a Bells.'

'Has Rodney paid you for the lunch yet?' I asked.

'Not yet, but he will. What happened to Julie?'

'I fear she has run off with Adam.'

'You can't blame her. Cheers!' He drank his whisky and studied the room thoughtfully.

'Perhaps they should have had children — they're supposed to preserve marriages,' I said. 'Did you ever have any?'

I could still see the shadow of the cricket pavilion in his sexual endeavours.

'Four with my first wife. Sue, Frank, Mark and Anna.'

'It sounds like a basket of currencies. What are you going to call the next one — Peseta?'

'There isn't going to be a next one,' he said. 'Or a next wife, by the look of it. They say that the ultimate result of all ambition is to be happy at home. That's a bloody laugh.' He continued to study the bar. 'You don't seem to pull many customers.'

'It's dinner time,' I told him. 'The bar will be crowded later.'

He nodded, satisfied, and then turned on his stool to face me. 'I'd like to buy it.'

'Why?'

'I've always fancied owning a small hotel, and the position of this one is perfect. I could have my own social centre, my own cronies, my own club. I could throw out my enemies.'

'Make me an offer,' I said.

I didn't think twice.

'I made you an offer yesterday.'

'An opening offer,' I said. 'Be serious.'

'Okay — three hundred and fifty thousand pounds.'

'It's yours.'

'Really?'

'You are the new owner of the Bali Hotel.'

'Why do you want to sell it?'

'It has . . . memories,' I told him.

The price was inflated wildly but neither of us was very impressed by that. When we were at school a £75,000 win on the football pools meant that you would never have to work again. Now I have several friends who earn that every two years. Soon we will all be millionaires but not able to afford a pint of beer, let alone a wristwatch television.

Chad was offering his hand over the bar to seal the deal and I shook it gladly. Laurel's letter was in the dustbin, Catchpole's sandwich bag was in the cellar, a pile of paperwork, that had built up over the weekend, was in the office, and my thoughts were rushing to escape from all of it.

'There's been a bit of *Sturm and Drang* this holiday,' I said. 'I need a break from it.'

Chad nodded sympathetically — he couldn't know of my attempt to turn the Bali Hotel into a corrective labour camp.

'I'll put the deal in motion tomorrow,' he said. 'Who are your solicitors?'

I told him and fetched myself a celebratory Scotch. It gave me a thought.

'You'll keep the staff, I hope?' I said. 'They are excellent.'

'Their jobs are safe,' said Chad. 'You can reassure them on that point. Give me another whisky, will you? It takes two drinks to get me where everybody else is the rest of the time.'

I put a large Scotch in his glass but refused his money: there would be enough of that heading for my bank account in the near future.

'Why didn't you ever get married, anyway?' he asked. 'You're not getting any younger, you know.'

I shrugged. 'Age may not bring wisdom, but it brings a certain weariness,' I said.

He finished the drink and stood up.

'You've got yourself a deal,' he said. 'I'll be in touch during the week.'

I sat alone with my glass and repeated £350,000 to myself, over and over again. I started to consider the things that a man could do with that sort of money, and the places that he could see. Only the previous day a lavish advertisement had invited me to step off the whitest beaches into rainforests that were strangely rich in primeval stirrings! I didn't know what it meant, but I liked the sound of it.

I was several thousand miles away — crossing the Bay of Bengal on my journey to a massage parlour in Bangkok — when the confidence trickster walked in.

One night that summer a middle-aged man in an absurdly checked suit had strolled into the bar and ordered a large whisky. He had the eyes of a cornered rat. The bar was fairly empty — it was the night of the Molly Malone seafood evening at the sailing club — and I found myself trapped in a conversation about racehorses. I have never been very interested in horses myself, although I have sometimes wondered

164

how they could convey that they had a headache and didn't wish to race or that, without spectacles, they couldn't see the jumps too clearly.

But this man, whose name — I was to regret afterwards — I never discovered, was full of information about the top jockeys, who were all, he assured me, personal friends, and he spoke knowledgeably about the best horses in training. It was Goodwood week and he was on his way home from the Stewards Cup.

He stood at the bar, ankle-deep in dropped names, and demanded another large whisky.

'You never back horses at all?' he asked.

'Never,' I told him.

'What's the most you ever won?'

A liar never believes anybody.

'I don't back them,' I repeated. 'I don't have the time to study form.'

'That's a pity. I make a lot of money at it.' He held up his large whisky as if in evidence of this alleged wealth. 'Matter of fact, I own a couple of horses. They're trained in Sussex.'

'Expensive business,' I said. I was wondering whether he would buy me a drink if I continued in the role of good listener.

'Matter of fact,' he said, 'one of them is running at Goodwood tomorrow.'

'Really?' I said. 'What's it called?'

He told me. It was Winter Day or Winter Morning or Winter something.

'Is it going to win?'

'Slowing down. It's got four lengths on the whole field.'

'What price is it?'

I couldn't see the bait until later; hindsight is an exact science.

'Twenty-five to one. Of course, it may come in a bit tomorrow. On the other hand, it may go out.'

The topic might have died there but he suddenly produced a *Sporting Life*, folded to show tomorrow's runners at Goodwood. There was Winter something, listed at a probable starting price of twenty-five to one. I had even heard of the jockey.

Why this should have impressed me as corroboration of what he had said, I don't know. He would have consulted his *Sporting Life* before he came in the bar.

'I ought to do it,' I said. 'But I don't have time to go into town.'

'Don't worry. I'll put it on for you. I'm coming back this way tomorrow.'

I took a twenty-pound note from my wallet and handed it to him.

The following evening I turned in to the racing results and wasn't at all surprised, given my inside information, to see that the horse had won at twenty to one. I went into the bar that evening and waited in vain for my four hundred pounds.

It was only afterwards that I realized that the man must have been confident that a twenty-five to one shot would lose, so that he would be able to come back having spent my money. A win like that lost him a customer.

But he walked in now in the same check suit as if no debt existed between us; perhaps he had arrived at the wrong hotel.

It was his lucky night. My feelings were now in such turmoil — guilt (Catchpole), remorse (Laurel), delight (Chad) — that only a liberal intake of Scotch was keeping me on a stable course. The guilt, the remorse and the delight, or any two from three, persuaded me that it was time I revealed a little generosity of spirit, even to a confidence trickster. After all, his crime was less than mine.

'What will you have, sir?' I asked.

He was still on large whiskies. He took the drink and looked round the bar as if he was trying to place it.

'How are your horses doing?' I asked. 'Still winning?'

He stared at me for a moment with his rat-like eyes and then the flicker of comprehension arrived, followed by the helpless flush of embarrassment. No rat ever felt so silly.

'I suppose they all win except for the creature I backed? Never mind.'

He spotted the escape with rodent guile. 'I'm afraid so,' he said. 'I can't win them all.' He was so uneasy I thought he would leave his drink. Clearly he had forgotten, until tonight, the day that he drove off with my foolishly offered twenty pounds in his fat wallet.

'I put your bet on — I remember it now — but the horse — what was it called?'

'Winter something.'

'Got beat.'

'Just my luck,' I said.

'You win some, you lose some,' he mumbled, emptying his glass quickly.

As he headed gratefully for the door Lisa arrived, and I left her to the bar and went through to the kitchen. I didn't feel as if I had eaten much today.

Scott was slicing a roast chicken and I stole a little and found some vegetables.

'I've been thinking,' he said, as I ate. 'How did that bloke get into the cellar if you had locked the door at the top of the stairs?'

I reflected that there were many more difficult questions that he could have posed.

'Well, he was obviously down there already, wasn't he?' I said. 'I locked him in, not knowing that he was there.'

'I see,' he said.

He looked as if another, more pertinent question was under consideration, but I knew how to erase this matter from his head.

'I've sold the hotel,' I told him.

'Oh, no,' he said, stopping work. 'You don't want to do that, Martin.' He didn't call me Martin very often. 'We've got a lovely set-up here.'

'I'm glad you think so. But time, like an ever-rolling stream . . .'

'Who have you sold it to? One of the big concerns?'

'No, an old schoolfriend of mine called Mr Cartwright. He doesn't want to change the staff. I don't think he wants to change anything. You'll hardly notice the difference.'

Judy came in.

'He's sold the Bali,' Scott told her.

She seemed distraught. 'No,' she whispered.

167

I suppose that I should have been flattered by their reaction, but I was already living in the future.

'You'll be all right, Judy,' I said. 'Your jobs are safe. He promised that.'

'You've ruined my evening,' she said, and went off to the bread cupboard.

As soon as I had eaten I hurried back to the bar. I had a taste for whisky this evening — and nights at the Bali had suddenly become a precious, numbered commodity.

Adam was sitting at the counter with a half-empty glass of bitter in front of him. He gave me a tired smile.

'I've had enough sex in the last twenty-four hours to last me at least until tonight,' he said.

'Where is all this venery going to get you?' I asked.

'Australia, pal.'

'Australia?'

'We're going this week if we can get a flight. We want to put a few miles between us and Rodney. We'll spend a month there and if we like it we're going to settle.'

'Julie has a cousin there,' I said, remembering.

'Yes, and she loves it.'

I don't know why I was surprised that Adam was heading for Australia, because I have known many men like him — restless, rootless and full of ideas — who have made the long journey south, never to be seen again.

'Are you going to marry her?' I asked.

He looked at me as if I had asked to borrow his sister for half an hour.

'Of course I'm going to marry her.'

'I thought marriage was a romance in which the hero died in the first chapter? I thought a husband was a bachelor whose luck ran out?'

'The trouble with you, pal, is that you're too cynical. You must have caught it from Mrs Stapleton.'

At the mention of her name she glided through the door, followed eagerly by her black labrador, Boz, whom she occasionally treated to a night out.

168

'Another Bacchanalian evening with the bourgeoisie,' she said, adjusting a stool. 'Sit, Boz!'

Boz jumped around, ignoring the injunction, and finally came to rest with both front paws on Adam's lap.

'Give me some crisps, Martin,' he said. 'Boz and I have an understanding. I buy him crisps and he doesn't accidentally castrate me.'

He opened the packet and threw the crisps into the air, while Boz displayed a remarkable repertoire of leaps and jumps.

'To ascend to the mundane,' said Mrs Stapleton, 'is there any prospect of getting a drink?'

I fetched a gin and gave it to her with Adam's news. She looked shocked.

'You can't do that,' she told him. 'I'll have no one to play with.'

'I'm only carrying out your advice, Alice,' said Adam. 'You said a good woman was what I needed.'

'I didn't say anything about going to the other side of the world. Where does the money come from?'

'Julie has money,' Adam said briefly.

'That's nice,' said Mrs Stapleton. 'Where is she, by the way?'

'Taking a shower, I believe.'

'You seem to spend half your time violating each other and the rest washing. Still, I'm glad you finally discovered sex.'

Adam beamed. 'Contrary to the impression you have of me, Alice, I've always been a bit of a performer. I had a burning in the groin at the age of thirteen.'

Mrs Stapleton raised a hand. 'Spare us your teenage inguinal temperatures, dear.'

Adam laughed happily and I was fascinated by the transformation in his personality. A sudden proximity to money had opened him up like a flower, and the glowering pessimism had disappeared.

I served myself another Scotch. Lisa was loading a tray for some drinkers who had been brought back to the patio by the sun. I was expecting a busy evening. The customers who had

169

chosen to spend their weekend away should be creeping back now to their normal routine — drinks in the Bali and a comfortable nine-to-five existence in Volvoland, as this area, through envy or condescension, is sometimes called.

But the next customer who came in was a rare visitor indeed. He was the vicar or curate at a tiny church up the lane. He appeared every Bank Holiday (except Good Friday) and drank a small lager. The survival of his church was one of God's mysteries, because I never heard of anybody who attended services there. I gave him his drink.

'Here comes the apostle of gloom,' said Mrs Stapleton. 'Good evening, vicar.'

'Good evening,' said the vicar, if he was a vicar. 'Doesn't this sun make you happy to be alive again?'

'I wouldn't go that far,' said Mrs Stapleton. 'It's all right for you. You know that your redeemer liveth.'

'You've put your finger on the truth of the matter as usual, Mrs Stapleton,' he said.

Boz was now begging for the lumps of cheese that he always enjoyed on his visits to the Bali, and I eased myself out of this company, the recidivist in their midst, and went to find some.

When I returned, Mrs Stapleton was saying, 'I've never understood Catholicism. The absurdity of seven hundred million people being told how to conduct their sex lives by a hundred eighty-year-old virgins living in another country is more than I can overlook.'

'We are not Catholics, Mrs Stapleton,' said the vicar. 'Your sex life is the last thing I wish to interfere with.'

'Yes, a lot of men seem to feel like that,' she said, and the vicar laughed. I quite liked him. If he had steeled himself to use the Bali more often he might have succeeded in transferring some of my congregation to his own premises on the hill.

When he had gone I decided that it was time to break my news. The bar had not filled up as I had expected; no doubt traffic jams were delaying the homecomings. Only Julie had

170

joined us at the bar, sipping bacardi and lemonade, and holding Adam's knee.

'Where are you going to in Australia?' Mrs Stapleton asked her.

'Rockhampton,' Julie said. 'It's on the east coast, north of Brisbane.'

'It's going to be pretty exciting for Adam,' I said. 'The farthest he has travelled so far is the Isle of Wight.'

'Apparently they talk English in Australia,' Adam said, 'so I'll be all right. Martin is naturally envious, stuck here in the sticks.'

'As a matter of fact, I won't be,' I said. 'I have sold the hotel to Chad Cartwright.'

'The man who paid for lunch yesterday?'

'The same.'

Mrs Stapleton put down her glass. 'I trust you are joking, Martin?'

'It's the truth,' I said. 'Pure and complex.'

'What on earth have you done that for?'

'I'm tired of worrying about tomorrow.'

'But tomorrow never comes, according to the song.'

'Tomorrow comes every bloody morning in this business.'

'It's a bit sudden, isn't it? First Adam, now you. My social life is disintegrating around me.'

'The Bali will still be here,' I said. 'I have just decided that it is time to move on.' The world only accepts you at your own valuation of yourself until it finds you out, I thought.

'That's terrible,' Mrs Stapleton said. She seemed to be genuinely sad and began to fondle Boz as if he, too, was planning to desert her. I was sorry that I couldn't give her the real reasons for my decision. The story of the body in the cellar had not yet spread, and the truth about it would never be revealed.

'Life goes on, Alice,' I said. 'Mr Cartwright will be as glad of your custom as I have been.'

'I think I need a large drink,' she said. 'At my age you don't like change.'

171

I filled all our glasses and paid for the drinks myself. Through the window I could see Denzil Kirby and Sharon, back from a waterlogged weekend in the New Forest, getting out of their car.

'Consider these facts, Adam,' said Mrs Stapleton. 'One, Martin is drinking whisky. Two, Laurel has disappeared. Three, Martin has sold the hotel. Where does it get us?'

'Yes, where is Laurel?' Julie asked.

'She has gone,' I told them.

'Do you mean the engagement is over?'

I nodded. 'It had dragged on for too long.'

'You only became engaged yesterday,' Mrs Stapleton said. 'Was it as long ago as that?'

'What's going on, Adam?' asked Mrs Stapleton. 'Do you know?' She turned to him, but he was engaged at that moment in kissing the tip of Julie's nose, an activity which seemed to have removed him from earshot.

'Nothing is going on,' I told her. 'I am no longer engaged. I am selling the Bali. I am enjoying a whisky.'

She put down the drink and frowned with concern.

'You *can't* sell the Bali, Martin,' she said, almost imploringly. 'You'll miss it. Besides, what will you do?'

I stared into my whisky glass, which was already empty, and thought: she is right. I shall miss it. I shall miss its friendly customers, its crazy evenings, its semi-malicious gossip and its sententious chatter. I shall certainly miss Alice Chetwynd Stapleton.

But I knew what I would do. When Chad's windfall materializes as countable sterling, I shall take it back to Maravillas, where rows of bars separate the palm trees from a two-mile beach. I shall buy one for myself, rename it The Cellar, and dispense gin fizzes and cuba libres to sun-burnt strangers.

I hear all the girls are topless there now. If I can find a good lettuce man it should be quite something.

THE END

BLESS ME AGAIN, FATHER
by Neil Boyd

"As bracing as a tot of Irish whiskey" *Yorkshire Telegraph and Argus*

The irrepressible trio from St Jude's are back!

It is Father Neil's second year in the Parish – but life is as hilarious and as chaotic as ever! Mrs Pring looks like accepting the hand of Billy Buzzle, the bookie from next door – Mother Stephen, the starchy Superior at the Convent threatens to denounce Father Neil for flirting with a policeman's wife – whilst Father Duddleswell, musing over whether he wouldn't have been better off if he'd become a Rabbi, suddenly learns that a bomb, dropped ten years ago, is about to blow up . . .

"Rollicking good humour . . . on a scale of ten, I'd put this one at laugh force nine" *Sunday Independent*

0 552 11903 2   £1.50

THE SECRET LEMONADE DRINKER
by Guy Bellamy

A RIBALD TALE OF BLONDES, BRUNETTES, BOOZE AND BOBBY BOOTH

"A major new comic talent . . . I laughed and I laughed, reading it in the state of tremulous excitement which must be the nearest we novel reviewers come to an understanding of heavenly bliss . . . the book is a corker – witty, intelligently observed, well written and original. Thank you Mr Bellamy."
Auberon Waugh, Evening Standard

"A very funny first novel . . . Bawdy, witty, sometimes touching, the book more than lives up to its zany title."
The Sun

"Guy Bellamy writes with gusto and panache and his cheerful, graphic sexual encounters are honestly sensuous. There's a touch of the Leslie Thomas here."
Newsagent and Bookshop

"Sparkling . . . It cracks open a thousand jokes, some old, some new and some blue . . . as hideously addictive as drink." *Sunday Times*

"One of the wittiest books I've read in years . . . a delicious book by a wonderfully funny, aphoristic writer." *Erica Jong*, author of FEAR OF FLYING

0 552 10796 4   £1.25

THE RUDE AWAKENING
by Brian W. Aldiss

The hilariously grim black comedy of men at war.

Superficially, Sergeant Stubbs is enjoying himself. Plump, sweet Margery has yielded to his repulsive charms and wants to marry him. He may even want to marry her, except that (the world being what it is) she isn't likely to be a lady. Then there's luscious Katie Chae – who's certainly not the marrying kind – not to mention . . .

Sweet success! But Stubbs has been rudely awakened to the fact that beneath the whoring and drunken parties there's a bitter reality . . . and that on the war-torn island of Sumatra death is as readily available as sex. This is the real, unvarnished world stripped, even in its language, to basics. Horatio can still see the funny side of it all, naturally . . . like a man whistling in the dark.

0 552 11142 2   95p

A SELECTION OF HUMOUR TITLES
AVAILABLE FROM CORGI BOOKS

While every effort is made to keep prices low, it is sometimes necessary to increase prices at short notice. Corgi Books reserve the right to show new retail prices on covers which may differ from those previously advertised in the text or elsewhere.

The prices shown below were correct at the time of going to press. (October 1983)

ORDER FORM

All these books are available at your book shop or newsagent, or can be ordered direct from the publisher. Just tick the titles you want and fill in the form below.

CORGI BOOKS, Cash Sales Department, P.O. Box 11, Falmouth, Cornwall.

Please send cheque or postal order, no currency.

Please allow cost of book(s) plus the following for postage and packing:

U.K. Customers—Allow 45p for the first book, 20p for the second book and 14p for each additional book ordered, to a maximum charge of £1.63.

B.F.P.O. and Eire—Allow 45p for the first book, 20p for the second book plus 14p per copy for the next seven books, thereafter 8p per book.

Overseas Customers—Allow 75p for the first book and 21p per copy for each additional book.

NAME (Block Letters) ....

ADDRESS ....

....